‘And what about us?’

Reece turned to face her head on, and Sorrel caught the merest glimpse of a muscle flexing slightly in the plane of his beautiful angled cheekbone and sensed the undoubted tension building inexorably inside him—as though he was on a very short fuse that was going to ignite any second now.

‘Us?’

‘Don’t you think it would do us both good to get away together? To have time to rest and relax and make some decisions about our future?’

Her heart jumped. *Hadn’t he already told her he was in this for ‘better or worse’? Was he now changing his mind?*

The day **Maggie Cox** saw the film version of *Wuthering Heights*, with a beautiful Merle Oberon and a very handsome Laurence Olivier, was the day that she became hooked on romance. From that day onwards she spent a lot of time dreaming up her own romances, secretly hoping that one day she might become published and get paid for doing what she loves most! Now that her dream is being realised, she wakes up every morning and counts her blessings. She is married to a gorgeous man, is the mother of two wonderful sons, and her two other great passions in life—besides her family and reading/writing—are music and films.

Recent titles by the same author:

MISTRESS ON DEMAND
THE ITALIAN'S PREGNANCY PROPOSAL

THE WEDLOCKED WIFE

BY
MAGGIE COX

To Tayyaba, from my heart to yours

First published in Great Britain 2006
Paperback Edition 2006
Harlequin Mills & Boon Limited,
Eton House, 18-24 Paradise Road, Richmond, Surrey TW9 1SR

ISBN 0 263 84804 3

Set in Times Roman 10½ on 12¾ pt.
01-0406-49303

Printed and bound in Spain
by Litografia Rosés, S.A., Barcelona

CHAPTER ONE

SORREL had been dreading this day. The almost absurdly formal room she'd been shown into seemed to echo her dread, and multiply her fear that nothing good could happen inside its singularly unwelcoming oak-panelled walls.

Despite it being the kind of glorious spring day outside that made a person glad to be alive, inside this forbidding room there was no such complementary feeling—no glimmer of hope or renewal at all. How could there be when Sorrel was about to come face to face with the husband she'd left three months ago and discuss their divorce?

Her stomach felt as if it had one huge knot inside it...had, in fact, been feeling like that for days now, with no relief. Absently, her fingers curled into her clothing, but they were so cold—as though they'd been plunged into ice—that they would hardly flex at all.

The thought of seeing Reece again filled Sorrel with one part joy and three parts sorrow. She'd always thought that their love was *unbreakable*...that it could withstand any rocky terrain or crashing wave that threatened to unbalance it. The last few months had tested that belief to the *limit*.

Reece had been a cold, unfeeling stranger to her the night she'd finally decided to leave him. An impenetrable stone eleventh-century castle wall couldn't have been more impervious. He'd been so caught up in the whirlwind of activity and demand that was his work that he simply hadn't even seemed to see that Sorrel had also had needs that were crying out to be met. Her husband had thought that *she* was the intolerant one—the one who was deliberately making difficulties where there really weren't any to begin with.

The following day, after the worst argument their marriage had ever endured, he'd left the house in the early hours of the morning to catch a train to York, to discuss a classical concert he was promoting, and Sorrel hadn't seen him at all. She'd told herself that if he'd cared sufficiently about repairing the damage that had been done between them he wouldn't have left to catch that train. He would have postponed his 'pressing and important' business meeting and stayed home, to attend to the far more important subject of his marriage. The fact that Reece hadn't done any such thing had left her with little alternative but to pack her bags and leave.

Disheartened and melancholy, Sorrel had moved out of the architect-designed house they'd shared in Pimlico, London, and temporarily moved in with her sister Melody and her family in Suffolk. She'd had to get away.

Everything had been getting her down…the rows, the hurt, the accusations, the horrible suspicions about who Reece spent his time with when he was away, and the long periods apart when time crawled by so deathly slow that Sorrel wanted to scream inside with loneliness. No amount of activity or socialising with friends could make up for the aching chasm deep inside her very soul that could only be made whole again by her husband's friendship and love.

She'd known when she'd married Reece that, being the internationally acclaimed music impresario he was, his job would naturally involve a lot of travel. Being a fashion model herself, Sorrel was not unused to travelling the world. But then had come the time when she'd stopped looking forward to boarding yet another plane or another private yacht and had simply longed to be home in her own place—a *real* home, with Reece. She couldn't explain it…she'd just suddenly needed to put down roots.

The rows had started when he had demonstrated no sign of wanting such simplicity at all. In fact, perversely, his work commitments had seemed to accelerate, and Sorrel had barely seen him from one week to the next—unless, of course, she'd travelled with him. Increasingly she had not wanted to do that.

'We'll have some coffee shortly, Mrs Villiers…we're just waiting for Mr Villiers to arrive. Are you comfortable? You look a little chilly, if you don't mind my saying. Shall I close the window?'

As the impeccably attired solicitor rose up from his seat at the head of the long formal table, Sorrel glanced up at him in alarm. 'No! Please don't shut the window.'

There was a real danger of her not being able to breathe if he shut out the vital supply of fresh spring air that just at that moment was helping her keep her anxiety at a level that was manageable. If he closed it off, the already daunting and chilly room would be even more like a tomb encasing her, and she wouldn't be able to sit still and face Reece across that alienating formal table and accept that he obviously didn't love her any more.

It was *he* who had instigated this discussion with his solicitor about a divorce. When Sorrel had received his letter at her sister's house a fortnight ago, she had wept until her eyes were dry of tears. She'd been hoping for an entirely *different* content in his coldly brief missive. Foolishly, and perhaps naively, she'd been hoping there might be talk of forgiveness and compromise…even starting over. *But it wasn't to be…*

Muted voices outside the door told her that her husband had arrived. Steeling herself for the sight of him, and unable to stop shivering at the prospect, Sorrel lifted her chin a little and silently prayed that she would not betray her distressing inner turmoil. *Why give him even more ammunition to shoot her down with than he had already?* This man had been her whole world, and now he was showing her that he no longer wanted to be part of her world at all. She almost couldn't bear it. She certainly didn't want him to see her devastation.

Just then he walked in the door, his heat-provoking glance immediately seeking her out, then frostily disregarding her as though she were an insignificant stranger. The stunning verdant gaze that had once studied her with such adoration now appeared as hostile as a sworn enemy…*as if love had never visited their captivating emerald depths at all…*

Sorrel didn't know how she remained in her seat instead of flying out through the door with grief.

'Welcome, Mr Villiers. Won't you sit down and make yourself comfortable? I will just have a word about some coffee for us all. Excuse me…'

Edward Carmichael—Reece's wealthy and dapper solicitor—made himself scarce from the room. Sorrel could feel the tension roll off her husband's impressive broad shoulders in almost tangible waves, and his formal grey pin-striped suit added to her already deepening sense of alienation and fear. She hardly knew what to say. In the end the dilemma was taken out of her hands.

'Did you drive into London?' Reece questioned her, his familiar transatlantic tones as formal as the lofty room that surrounded them.

'No, actually, I didn't. I came up on the train. I was going to drive, but then I—I decided against it in case the traffic was bad.' Self-consciously, Sorrel's words died away. She'd been about to explain that she'd been suffering from an upset stomach for the past few days and had worried about being carsick. But then she thought better of revealing such an intimate detail to her husband, because she was afraid to witness his undoubted lack of concern. 'Anyway…' She shrugged her shoulders in the butter-soft tan suede jacket she wore over her knitted cardigan, feeling ill with nerves. The sheer strain of the past three months and her dread of what the future might hold had taken its toll. 'At least I was able to read my book on the train.'

Drawing out the high-backed chair opposite her, Reece undid the buttons on his suit jacket and sat down. 'Hopefully we can get this over with as quickly and as painlessly as possible,' he remarked, reaching out to pour some water from the carafe in front of him into a cut crystal tumbler.

Did he *really* hope that? Then it was clear that he must possess a heart of stone, Sorrel thought in despair. Her hurt blue eyes considered the aloofly handsome face before her, with its clean-cut and strongly defined symmetry of jaw and cheekbone, the slight cleft in his indomitable chin that she'd always found so disarmingly sexy, and the piercingly sharp intelligent green eyes that complemented his dark blond hair. It was hard to believe that he'd once told her that she was the woman of his dreams. Now he looked at her as if he could hardly bear to be in the same room as her!

'I—I didn't expect to get such a letter from you,' she forced herself to say, needing to make a more personal connection—even if it was a somewhat wounded one. But just then the solicitor returned, followed by a woman bearing a tray with coffee. She deposited it between Reece and Sorrel then discreetly left. Edward Carmichael resumed his seat, settled his hands on the blotter in front of him and cleared his throat.

Reece's heart and stomach had seemed simultaneously to somersault at the sight of his arrestingly beautiful young wife. He was quite aware that he'd spent a large part of their two-and-a-half-year-old marriage away, travelling for his work, but the last eleven weeks and two days had seemed like an eternity without her. At least when he had been away before Reece had always known that he had Sorrel to come home to. Now the stunning state-of-the-art house he had had constructed just for her seemed like a glass and steel prison without her in it. A *luxurious* glass and steel prison, full of expensive furniture and *objets d'art*—rooms empty of anyone to appreciate them or even use them. Because being in the house for any time at all was a too-painful reminder of what Reece had lost.

But, even so, he couldn't gaze upon Sorrel's blond angelic perfection with any genuine delight or pleasure any more. The woman had walked out on him and left him, clearly demonstrating her contempt. She hadn't even had the decency to leave him a goodbye note. Instead, her partially denuded wardrobe and two missing suitcases had testified to the fact that she'd gone away, and in three long months Reece had had neither letter or phone call to let him know how she was or what she intended to do about their clearly disintegrating relationship.

He had tortured himself with the possibility that she might have met someone else, was having an affair and hadn't been able to confess to him the true reason that she had left him.

Sorrel's closest relationship outside of their marriage had always been with her sister Melody, so Reece had been in no doubt that she'd gone there. After ringing and checking that that was the case, and being reassured by Melody that Sorrel *definitely* wasn't seeing anyone else, Reece had had to force himself to come to terms with her absence.

Furious that she had eliminated the chance for him to express his feelings on her leaving, Reece had decided to wait no longer for Sorrel to make a decision. Instead he'd called her bluff and decided that a quick and easy divorce was probably the best solution all round. Why wait when all they had done for months now was argue anyway?

Reece was sick of it. He'd never dreamt in a million years that the slightly self-effacing, calm, even-tempered angel he'd married could make his life quite so difficult or inflame his temper more quickly than anyone or anything else. The tense situation between them had started to infringe upon Reece's work, too, tearing his mind away from it when his job required all the concentration he could muster. But he'd found it increasingly hard to detach himself emotionally and focus on business when most of his thoughts seemed to be concerned with Sorrel. Seeing her again now, after nearly three months, wasn't making things any easier…

'Shall we proceed?'

Bestowing his best professional smile on both of them in turn, the unctuous Edward Carmichael straightened some papers on the blotter in front of him, clearly denoting that *he* was the one their attention should be focused on, and *not* each other.

His hands were small and very white, Sorrel noticed—with perfectly manicured nails and a thick gold wedding ring encasing one plump little finger. She turned her head forlornly away at the sight of it, suddenly wishing that she hadn't removed the slim platinum band that Reece had put on her finger on their wedding day only this morning, before Melody had driven her to the station to catch her train. Sorrel had only done it because she'd suddenly had the crazy idea that he might ask for it back. Now she saw that Reece might justifiably interpret her not wearing it as agreement to his suggestion that they end their marriage.

Guiltily, she covered the offending hand with its opposite one in her lap. She *didn't* want this divorce. She'd *never* wanted things between her and Reece to go this far or get this bad. If only she had relented and spoken to him when he'd rung Melody, or at least contacted him herself soon after she'd left to suggest they get together and talk about their troubles like civilised human beings—they might have stood a chance of repairing the damage. Instead she'd stubbornly stayed silent and uncommunicative in the stupidly vain hope that *he* would contact her first and say sorry.

He'd said some terrible things to her that awful night, when they'd had the row to end all rows. His words had been like razor-sharp swords flailing through her heart, slicing it to shreds. Nursing her wounds, Sorrel had longed for Reece to be the one to make the first step towards reconciling. Lifting her gaze to study his expression on the other side of the table, she saw to her great pain that he appeared no less remote and no more amicable than he had when he'd first come through the door. *He obviously couldn't wait to cut the ties that bound them together for good.*

'If you wouldn't mind,' she heard him say in answer to the solicitor's suggestion, 'I'm catching a train to Edinburgh in a couple of hours, so I'd appreciate it if we could move things along fairly quickly.'

That was when Sorrel literally smelled the coffee. The strong aroma made her stomach roll, then frighteningly threaten to relieve her of her breakfast. Before either Edward Carmichael or Reece had a chance to react, she leapt to her feet and dashed out through the door, calling out to the smartly attired woman on the reception desk for directions to the nearest ladies' toilet.

Running down a long black-and-white checked marble floor which oddly made her think of that strange game of chess in *Alice in Wonderland*—Sorrel swept towards the destination she was seeking in double-quick time, barely making it into the nearest cubicle before she was wretchedly and horribly sick.

It was several long minutes before her insides calmed down and she risked returning to the solicitor's office. When she did, her face was almost as chalk-white as one of the smooth marble busts to be found in any museum, and her limbs felt no stronger than fragile sheaves of corn.

Reece was on his feet the moment she entered, his expression grimly concerned.

'Are you all right? What the hell happened?'

Automatically he'd come over to her and put his hand behind her waist, to lead her back to the chair she had so abruptly vacated. Sorrel knew that if she dared reply at that moment it might open the floodgates on her tears, and she would embarrass herself in front of her husband and his solicitor all over again. All she longed for, all she really wanted, was for Reece to put his arms around her and tell her that he was taking her *home*.

But she and Reece didn't even share a home any more, she painfully reminded herself—and probably wouldn't again after the outcome of this meeting. So her longing would have to go unanswered.

'It was just the stupidest thing…the smell of the coffee, that's all. It's never happened before. I'm sorry.'

Sorrel didn't see Reece's own face practically drain of colour. Returning to his seat, he didn't sit down but formidably remained standing. His commanding presence was even more riveting in this solemn, almost funereal room. She gazed up at him in genuine bewilderment.

'What's the matter?'

'Did it even occur to you that you might be pregnant, Sorrel?' he asked, emerald eyes glittering hard.

The truth hit her like a thunderbolt shooting out of the sky. The queasy churning stomach she had had for days now; the acute tingling sensation in her breasts; the need to have all the windows opened in whatever room she was in else otherwise she'd feel as if there wasn't enough air to breathe. Never having been pregnant before, Sorrel had put all those symptoms down to the fact that she was mourning her doomed relationship. She'd been heartsick and in despair, because despite everything—the rows, the tension, the sometimes seemingly relentless periods of deep unhappiness—she loved Reece almost more than life itself.

And her periods had never been completely reliable anyway. Two or three months could easily go by without her having one or being alarmed by the fact. *But the night before the row to end all rows she and Reece had loved each other long into the night.* And because he'd been away for a whole month, and their need for each other had almost been bordering on desperate—in spite of their marital difficulties—they hadn't given a thought to using protection…

'I'm—I'm not! I can't be!'

Helplessly she glanced across at Edward Carmichael, who had linked his perfectly manicured hands together and was frowning deeply—just like a prosecutor in a medieval court, having just found Sorrel guilty of witchcraft.

Her voice rose. 'I've just had a bit of an upset stomach, that's all!'

'Have you seen a doctor?'

His voice still sounding remote, as though nothing would ever make it warm towards her ever again, Reece kept his piercing gaze focused on Sorrel's stricken face.

'No. Why should I have? I was—I was upset about all this…about us. I didn't think it was due to anything else.'

She was stunned, the full impact of the possibility of pregnancy starting to permeate her brain.

'I think under the circumstances that I should leave you two to talk, Mr Villiers.'

Rising to his feet, the solicitor glanced reprovingly from one to the other.

'Take as long as you like. Just tell my receptionist when you're ready to see me again.'

As the door closed firmly shut behind him, Reece didn't quite know what to do with the plethora of strong emotion that was running wildly through his veins. *Sorrel was pregnant.* He needed a moment for the idea to sink in. She was going to have a baby. His heart felt as if it was on a white-water ride, hurtling towards inevitable rapids. It was very *definitely* heading into even more dangerous waters when a new and unwelcome thought ruthlessly impinged itself upon his already assaulted mind.

'Is it mine?' he demanded, his tone furious and condemning.

Her gaze didn't waver for even an instant from her husband's angry yet undoubtedly handsome face, but the hurt that his cruel reaction engendered momentarily sucked all the breath from her lungs—like the wave of heat that hit mercilessly when you stepped out of an air-conditioned hotel lobby onto the baking pavements of Crete or Rome.

'I can't believe you would ask me such a dreadful question. Of course it's yours! Are you suggesting that I've been seeing someone else behind your back? What are you trying to do? Make a mockery of our entire marriage?'

'Right now I don't know what to think. I thought I knew you, Sorrel, but I was wrong. That all changed when you walked out on me three months ago.'

Shocked at the bitterness that was lacing his accusing tone, Sorrel shook her head slowly from side to side. 'And you don't think that might have anything to do with the selfish, unreasonable and totally stubborn way you've been acting? You'd rather believe I left you because I was seeing another man than imagine for even for one second that any blame might lie at your own door? I walked out on you, Reece, because I was sick of being made to feel like a second-class citizen in this marriage! The psychologists are right when they say it takes two to make a relationship work. As far as I can see all you've ever been concerned with is doing what *you* want to do, and my needs and wants can go hang!'

'That's a damn lie, and you know it!' Scraping his fingers harshly through his hair, uncaringly dislodging its previous order, Reece glared at her. 'What the hell are you complaining about? Anyone would think you had difficult circumstances to contend with! We live in the lap of luxury, Sorrel. You have the opportunity to travel the world on a regular basis. I'm not asking you to stay at home and live in squalor while I try and earn a crust—all I've ever asked is that sometimes you travel with me so that I can spend time with you. Is that so damn unreasonable?'

'And what about *you* staying in our home sometimes, and spending time with *me*? When you're travelling you can't make a proper home, and I told you that I need that. I need to put down roots—not just be aimless!'

'You knew what I did for a living when we met. You thought it was glamorous and exciting then. You also knew the demanding hours I had to work and you accepted them…or at least you seemed to. As far as your own career was concerned, you said yourself your heart wasn't in it, and I don't blame you—but it must have occurred to you somewhere along the line that I wasn't the kind of guy who could easily stay at home and play happy families with you, Sorrel, so don't act like some innocent injured party who didn't know the score!'

Nothing had changed. Three months apart and Reece clearly had developed no intention or even any desire to discuss what Sorrel wanted. That was why the only solution to the stalemate they had reached was to instigate divorce proceedings. *He was right and she was wrong.*

For a moment Sorrel had forgotten the added dilemma that she now faced—the fact that she was quite likely pregnant with their child. Nothing was working out as she'd hoped. When she'd allowed herself a fantasy about having children, she'd always dreamed that news of her pregnancy would be greeted with joy from her husband. Faced with the reality of her situation now, nothing could be further from that hope.

Sorrel was heartbroken for her child. To be a newly born infant of divorced parents who couldn't reconcile their differences…*how tragic*. Her throat threatened to close with pain; her soft blue eyes could not hide her hurt and distress.

'And what about the baby?'

She prayed he wasn't going to suggest the unthinkable. Reece would be an utter stranger to her if he did. Whatever his opinion, Sorrel was determined she was going to keep her baby and raise it on her own—no matter *what* she had to do.

Presenting her with his back, her husband slid one hand into his trouser pocket and strode thoughtfully away from her. Pausing for a moment, as if he needed to be clear in his own mind about what he was about to propound, he turned back to face her, as if reaching a conclusion that met all the rigours of his brief but razor-sharp investigation.

'The baby changes everything,' he told her, his voice resolute.

CHAPTER TWO

'WHAT do you mean?' Her voice strained with nerves, Sorrel's hand instinctively strayed to the still flat plane of her stomach beneath the brown cotton chinos she wore with her cardigan and jacket.

'I mean that now there will be no divorce.'

'You're changing your mind because of the baby?'

'What else did you expect? Whatever my feelings are towards you, Sorrel, I have no intention of walking off into the sunset and turning my back on the child. Did you imagine for even one second that I would still divorce you under the circumstances?'

She hated his coldness. Hated and feared it. What kind of a home could their precious baby have if there was no harmony there? If their father no longer loved their mother but instead *despised* her?

Getting to her feet, Sorrel felt her limbs were weighted down by sorrow. Brushing a trembling hand through the shimmering fall of her soft blond hair, she wished she didn't feel so vulnerable and afraid. Yet beneath her fear and vulnerability she sensed a new strength of purpose flood her being. Reece was not going to have everything his way. She would fight for her child's and her own happiness as long as she had breath inside her, and until she could make things right again for them both.

'It's not just your decision Reece,' she heard herself state clearly. 'If I decide that I don't want to stay married to you then nothing you say or do can change my mind.'

'If you *don't* stay married to me, Sorrel, then there is no way on this earth that you're going to keep me out of the picture and get full custody of our child. I'd take you to every court in the land if I had to… Am I getting through to you?'

'Is that some kind of a threat?'

Her chest had never felt so tight with dread, and she stared at Reece in alarm and disbelief, hardly recognising him as the man she loved. 'Are you telling me that you'd actually take me to court to get custody of our baby?'

He shrugged his wide muscular shoulders, as if her shocked question barely needed an answer it was so obvious.

'What do *you* think? Do I strike you as a passive bystander, Sorrel? Surely you know me better than that? My wealth can buy me the best damn legal representation in the country, and I won't hesitate to employ it if you even make the smallest move towards filing for divorce. In contrast, apart from a little part-time modelling, you're effectively a woman without regular employment or recourse to money except for what I give you. Who do you think has the strongest case? Think about it. And while you're thinking I'll go and find my attorney to tell him that I've changed my mind about the divorce. After that I'm driving you back to Suffolk to pick up your things and bringing you back home.'

'But why would you take me to court for custody of our child when you've already made it perfectly clear that you're not interested in staying at home and playing "happy families," as you so disdainfully put it?'

He seemed to consider her words for a long moment, and then answered her, barely demonstrating even the most fleeting flicker of emotion. 'Women don't have a prerogative on changing their minds, Sorrel. Now that you're pregnant I have to face facts, and the facts are that I helped create that baby in your womb and therefore I have a duty to help raise him. Do you think I'd just let you walk away and bring up the child on your own? Did you seriously believe for even a moment that I wouldn't have something to say about that?'

Swallowing across the pain in her throat, Sorrel felt her head swim with unhappiness. 'I'm not without recourse to money!' she told him, stung. 'I can get more regular modelling work if I choose to—just like that—' she clicked her fingers '—tomorrow!'

'But for how long? You're pregnant, remember?'

Furious crimson surged into her cheeks. 'I'm not coming back to Pimlico with you, Reece. I want to stay in Suffolk with Melody.'

'You don't have a choice, Sorrel. Your last option ran out when I found out that you're carrying my baby. You're coming home with me and that's all there is to it.'

'But you said you had to catch a train to Edinburgh! Surely you're not going to break a lifetime's habit and put off one of your precious meetings just for me?'

Throwing her a frosty, almost contemptuous glance over his shoulder, Reece wrenched open the door with force. 'All my plans are on hold until you are back where you are supposed to be,' he told her icily.

'Who do you think you are, telling me where I'm "supposed" to be? I make my own decisions about that, for your information! I'm a grown woman, and where I want to be is with my sister in Suffolk…not with you!'

He made a brief about-turn at her angry declaration. Raising one disdainful dark blond eyebrow, he curved his lips upwards in a sardonic grin. 'You are *my* wife, Sorrel, expecting *my* child, and any judge in the world will quickly and rightly deduce that in terms of your best interests—yours and the child's—your place is with me. End of discussion.'

Before Sorrel could utter another word, either in protest or in her own defence, Reece had exited the room and shut the door firmly behind him….

She stood in the bedroom, gazing out through the slatted glass doors at the perfectly square roof terrace with its huge terracotta pots rioting with spring blooms, and the trailing ivy drifting across the whitewashed stone walls that stood behind them. There was a chrome table and chair set arranged in a central position on the smooth marble tiled floor. Everything appeared precision-perfect and untouched. Just as though it was waiting expectantly for a photographer from one of those stylish homes magazines to come and capture it for next year's spring edition. Just the way it had appeared on the morning Sorrel had packed her bags and left.

Apart from the gorgeous pinks, yellows and blues of the cascading flowers, it seemed even more soulless and unappealing to her jaundiced gaze than ever. She told herself that she might have viewed it with some pleasure if she had returned home under completely different and more unified circumstances with Reece. But how could she view this cold showpiece house as a home at all when her relationship with her husband was about as amicable as two prize-fighting boxers stepping out into the ring for the championship title?

'Well?'

The sound of his voice startled her as he came into the room behind her. Sorrel knew instantly what he was asking. He wanted to know the result of the home pregnancy test she had purchased from the chemist on their way back home from Suffolk. Part of her wanted to lie to him…to do anything she could to delay giving him an answer, so furious and hurt was she at his unyielding and frighteningly bitter attitude towards her. As if she was some kind of criminal instead of the woman that loved him.

Slowly she turned around to face him, her arms folded protectively across her chest, subconsciously sending out a signal that this was her space and he'd better not transgress it.

'It was positive.'

Inhaling deeply, Reece mentally steadied himself. It took every ounce of the iron-clad determination he had in him not to go to his wife, persuade her down onto the big double bed positioned mockingly between them and make love to her with all the desire, need and desperation in his body. Just because she'd done the worst thing she could possibly do in leaving him, it didn't mean that Reece had stopped physically desiring her.

Sorrel was the only woman he'd ever met in his thirty-nine years he'd known on sight he wanted to marry. The only woman he could envisage spending the rest of his life with. Becoming a father might not have been part of his immediate future plans, but he would stand by his wife and child and provide for them as conscience dictated. No amount of protest or resistance from Sorrel would prevent him from meeting his responsibilities with all the rigour and attention to detail that he applied to everything in his life to keep things running smoothly.

Still, he took no pleasure in the thought of what the future might bring. They should have been enjoying completing two and a half years of blissful marriage and looking forward to more of the same. Instead a situation had arisen that could only help make Reece's relationship with his wife more brittle and remote than ever. *And he wasn't about to easily forgive her for walking out on him either.*

When she had left, Reece's fury had known no bounds. It didn't matter that he'd guessed almost immediately that she had gone to her sister's, or that he'd made Melody swear that she would contact him if Sorrel were in any kind of difficulty or need whatsoever. It hadn't stopped him from feeling devastated that she had walked out on their marriage without even giving him a chance to make recompense. So, even though she now found herself pregnant with their child, Reece's resentment towards her had not softened one iota.

He had waited a long time to fall in love, and he hadn't been in a hurry. There were some things in life definitely worth waiting for and in Reece's opinion Sorrel Claiborne had been one of them. When he'd seen her walk through the door at a post-performance party in a popular London theatre three years ago—even though she'd been on the arm of another man—Reece had felt desire crash through him with such force that it had almost knocked him off his feet.

She'd been breathtakingly lovely, in a gauzy pink camisole and skirt, one of the spaghetti straps of her top every now and again slipping down over one perfectly smooth pale shoulder, giving Reece a provocative glimpse of the gentle swell of her breast. But it had been her face, her honest-to-God, heartstoppingly beautiful face, that had captured his attention and kept it that night. In his opinion, artists and make-up companies alike should have been breaking down her door in droves to get her to model for them with such a face.

The fact that now Reece appeared to be seeing all his hopes and dreams where she was concerned turn into bitter dust was something he was just going to have to learn to live with. Sorrel would remain his wife. He was *adamant* about that, whatever the current state of his feelings towards her. And, as far as parenthood went, there was no question that they wouldn't make the best job of it that they could—even if their personal relationship could never be what it might have been.

Wiping his hand across his brow, Reece sighed with relief that at least decisions were being made and that to some extent the deadlock between them had been broken. Even if those decisions didn't immediately suit his errant wife.

'You'll have to get a medical check-up with your GP—that's the next thing. Leave it to me. I'll see to it.'

Sorrel's eyes stung from her determination not to cry. She fiercely pushed down the need that arose inside her to beg him to hold her, to forgive her for walking out and not letting him know that she was OK, to swallow her stupid pride and at least make some move towards a compromise even if Reece wouldn't. *They were going to have a baby.* If ever there was reason to bring some love back into their situation then surely this was it?

But as Sorrel saw the distance in Reece's glance become wider and deeper than one of the world's vast oceans, the words she longed to be able to say stayed unhappily locked inside her heart. She squared her shoulders, preparing to take more caustic mental blows. 'I can do that myself. I know you doubt my ability to function without your guidance, but even *I*—feeble-brained woman that I am—know how to punch out a number on a phone and make a doctor's appointment!'

'Let's not turn this into another slanging match, Sorrel. It really doesn't matter *who* makes the damn doctor's appointment as long as it gets made! It's not some master plan I have to try and control you! Getting checked over by the doctor is the sensible and right thing to do. You don't take unnecessary risks where something like a pregnancy is concerned. I only want to make sure that you and the baby get the proper attention you deserve.'

He shrugged his shoulders—the wide, impressive kind that any woman young or old would love the opportunity to cry on—his whole demeanour denoting frustration and anger. Just as though he'd resigned himself to never expecting any kind of softness or tenderness from Sorrel ever again. The sorrow that created in his wife's heart was immeasurable.

'What are you implying?' she asked, unable to keep her resentment at bay despite her sadness. 'That I might do something to hurt myself or my baby just to get back at you in some way?'

'Stop being so paranoid! I'm not saying that at all. I simply want to remind you that we're in this together, and I don't intend to stand on the sidelines and see you struggle through it on your own.'

'Oh? Since when did you care about me doing things on my own?' Sorrel's mouth twisted with unhappiness. 'Let's get one thing clear from the start, Reece. I've no illusions about having to cope with this pregnancy on my own. You'll be away working, just like you're *always* away working, and I'll simply have to get on with it like I usually do. Don't pretend that it's going to be any different because you've just found out that you're going to be a father!' Her slender shoulders slumped a little and a shadow of pain seemed to pass across the dazzling blue of her irises. 'And I've no doubt that when the baby comes not much will change for you there either. Except this time there'll be two of us waiting at home for you to deign to remember we exist.'

'Now you're being ridiculous! OK, so neither of us actually planned this baby, but now that it's clear we're going to be parents I fully intend to be as good a father as I can be to my son or daughter. I can't believe that you'd think otherwise…but then I obviously give you far more credit than you deserve.'

He had a way of looking at her sometimes that could make her feel very small, and every time he employed it Sorrel was crushed. Unfolding her arms, she dropped them down by her sides. *The situation was impossible.* Her leaving had done nothing but make matters worse. Her husband was clearly harbouring massive resentment that she had dared to walk out on him because she was so unhappy, and now that she was expecting his baby he saw it as the perfect opportunity to bring her back into line again and make her pay for her actions. Sorrel really didn't think she had it in her to survive mentally or emotionally under such acrid circumstances.

'I want you to know that I've moved back here completely reluctantly and totally against my better judgement. I'm here because I can't risk you being so bitter and twisted that you'd seriously take me to court to gain custody of our child. I also want you to know that I will fight for my baby's happiness *and* my own. So don't think that just because I'm home again you're going to have it all your own way!'

'Are you quite finished?'

Employing a look of boredom and disdain, Reece barely tolerated Sorrel's impassioned words, and for a moment his glance threatened her ability to proceed. But then she swallowed down the horrible aching cramp in her throat that was making it so difficult to give full vent to her feelings and stared back at him defiantly.

'You've got your work…you've *always* had your work…and I know perfectly well that that's always going to come first. And, just so that you're aware, I have other opportunities apart from modelling in which to earn money—and I'll certainly be taking advantage of them while I live in this house. I don't expect you to keep me. I never have! It was you who suggested I take fewer and fewer modelling assignments, so that I could travel around with you and keep you company while you pursued your own career. So don't think you hold the trump card just because you're the one who pays the bills!'

'This is crazy.' She saw the disdain in his eyes swiftly replaced by rage. 'There's absolutely no need for you to work at all, so you can put that idea right out of your head this instant! You're pregnant, remember? Naturally you're going to need as much rest and relaxation as possible in your condition. So don't be stupid about this, Sorrel. It won't solve a damn thing.'

It was clear that Reece was in no mood for examining solutions to their seemingly escalating animosity towards each other. And Sorrel too was in a space where calm logic and cool reason were nowhere to be found. How could she apply any such reasonable behaviour when her emotions about Reece and the baby were dominating her every thought?

'If you want to keep yourself occupied,' he continued, 'you can resume your yoga or Pilates classes, go to the spa, take up cross-stitch or any damn thing you like to keep you busy, if that's what you want, but there's no need for you to work. I'll double your allowance and you can do what the hell you like with the money—you know damn well you've never had to report back to me about what you spend! Let's just try and make things as bearable as possible while we're waiting for the baby to be born. After that...' Reece shrugged again, his handsome face looking suddenly weary. 'We'll see.'

As he turned towards the open doorway Sorrel's chest grew tight with anxiety. 'What do you mean "we'll see"?'

she demanded, her blue eyes flashing. But Reece was already gone and her indignant retort went ominously unanswered.

Melody had not professed instant happiness that Sorrel was pregnant.

'This is probably the last thing the two of you need when you're already in such a mess!' she declared in her usual forthright tone on the other end of the phone.

Sorrel had a brief flash of her driving her fingers through the thick wavy fair hair that could never be easily contained with undisguised exasperation. Of the two sisters, Melody had always been the practical, reliable one. A true lynchpin in the little Suffolk village community where she lived—the first to help sort out a neighbour's problem or run half a dozen of her friends' children to school as well as her own at the drop of a hat—nothing fazed her. Whether it came to baking her own bread, or changing a tyre on her dusty well-used Renault, Melody simply got on with the task at hand and didn't make a fuss. Apart from her sister being her closest friend, Sorrel had gone to her when she'd left Reece because Melody was bound to know what to do.

'I really do want this baby, Mel,' Sorrel replied now, wanting to make it clear that, in spite of the situation between herself and Reece, her baby would be very much loved and cared for.

'Of course you do, darling! But the fact remains that your timing stinks! What has Reece got to say about all this?'

Sorrel didn't like to reveal that they were barely talking. Two wounded strangers sharing a stunning 'magazine cover' house—going through the motions of a relationship that was clearly failing at every turn. The realisation made her feel both ashamed and a failure—especially when Melody's ten-year-old marriage to her stockbroker husband Simon was still thriving.

'He wants to do what's right,' she replied quietly, catching a sudden sight of her pale, anxious reflection in the glass of the patio doors that led onto the terrace. *God, she looked like a ghost!*

'Of course he does! He might be wrapped up in his career a bit too much, but the man has never lacked integrity. You walking out on him really hurt him, Sorrel. It's only natural that he's going to be angry with you for a while, but eventually he'll come round. He loves you, darling…you'll see.'

'I wish I had your confidence.'

Running her fingers along the polished surface of the maplewood cabinet in the hall, Sorrel absentmindedly examined their tips for dust. Finding none, she let her hand drop to her side. 'He's been angry at me for the whole of the past year, and I don't see any sign of it waning just yet. Even with the baby coming…'

'Well, if it all gets too much you can always come back to me for a break. Daisy and Will keep asking, "When are we going to see Auntie Sorrel again, Mummy?" and, "Why aren't you as pretty as she is, Mummy? Were you the black sheep of the family?"'

Sorrel laughed out loud—a genuine welling of affection in her heart for her little nephew and niece. 'They do say the funniest things, don't they? You should tell them that Auntie Sorrel might be pretty, but their mummy is the most beautiful and accomplished woman in the whole of Suffolk!'

'Well, as long as Simon thinks so I'm not complaining. I'm serious, though, darling. Just hang on in there, and if the going gets too tough you know where I am, don't you?'

After speaking to her sister, Sorrel made an appointment with her doctor and then telephoned her parents in Australia with her news. Having not given them the slightest hint that her marriage was in trouble at any point—not even when she'd moved out to stay with Melody—Sorrel tried to sound appropriately elated. *It was so hard.* Especially when her mother's highly emotional and happy response threatened to open the floodgates on her own emotions. And when she finally got to speak to her father, Charles Claiborne started to enthuse over plans to come to the UK in the summer for an especially long visit—to see his two beloved girls and, of course, the grandchildren that he'd been missing so much.

Instead of feeling her spirits lifted by speaking to her parents, Sorrel's mood plummeted even lower. In the face of their apparent joy about their expected grandchild, her own deep unhappiness seemed even more heartbreaking and unresolvable than ever.

Reece was in the huge house somewhere—probably working in his office, she suspected. No change there, then, as far as *his* priorities were concerned. So she was left yet again to find an occupation to fill the empty hours that stretched towards the warm spring evening.

Her mind naturally turned to her future. Feeling even

more defiant than ever at her husband's insistence that he didn't want her to work whilst she was pregnant, she went to her room and carefully extracted the large portfolio of fashion drawings she had been working on for some time now. She'd tentatively shown them to a dress designer friend of hers who had an exclusive shop in Chelsea, and Nina had been genuinely astonished at the talent she'd insisted Sorrel's sketches displayed.

In her five years of fashion modelling—up until she'd married Reece—Sorrel had naturally made quite a few useful contacts in the world of couture fashion. Nina Bryant was just one of them. With her friend's encouragement, she was determined to take advantage of all the contacts she could, and perhaps gain some useful employment for her supposed talents.

Her need to be independent again after the hurtful things that Reece had said to her would be the drive she needed to prepare for life after the baby came. Because, no matter how much he believed he had a hold on her—because he was the one with the wealth and she should be too scared to leave in case the courts gave him full custody—Sorrel needed to have a 'fallback' should the situation between them get any worse. Even if she struggled financially—and she prayed she wouldn't have to—surely it would be better than living with a man who had clearly fallen out of love with her? His only reason for staying married to her was that they were to have a child together, and he wouldn't rescind on his innate sense of responsibility....

CHAPTER THREE

HAVING made reservations at his favourite restaurant for dinner, Reece consulted his over-full diary as he sat at his desk in his study, and proceeded to cancel and rearrange as many appointments as he could over the next few weeks. His overriding emotion towards his young wife might predominantly be anger because of what she'd done, but he still harboured enough affection to be concerned about her.

The moment he'd seen her in the solicitor's office he had noticed that she had lost a little weight, and there was a distinct sense of defeat about her shoulders that Reece couldn't help but feel responsible for. He'd always been concerned that Sorrel didn't take care of herself enough. Her job dictated that she regularly had to curtail her appetite to stay as willowy and slender as she was, and Reece hadn't always liked that. That was one of the reasons he'd wanted her to give up modelling when he met her—his desire and hope that she would just be able to eat normally like any other healthy young girl.

He'd loved the notion of taking her to all the most wonderful places in the world to eat and witnessing her enjoyment, and in their first year of marriage together he had done exactly that. But that seemed like a long time ago now, and Reece could hardly bear to reflect on the happiness they'd shared then and consider in contrast what trouble they were in now.

Raising the pretty silver-framed photograph on the desk in front of him to examine it more closely, Reece studied the portrait of his wife that always made his heart beat a little faster—no matter how many times he glanced at it. There was a smaller version of the same picture in his wallet, and whenever he was away from Sorrel not a day went by when he didn't take it out to look at it. *The past three months hadn't been any different.* Her bewitching face was equal parts angel and enchantress—those distinctly almond-shaped baby blue eyes of hers unusual enough and striking enough to make you take a second glance even if the rest of her hadn't been as equally beautiful or striking.

He'd felt so damn *lucky* when he'd married her—knowing that other men would always look at him with her and envy his good fortune. And besides her delightful looks there had just been so much about Sorrel to love. Even though she'd been an up-and-coming young fashion model when Reece had first met her, she had never been one of those women that needed constant high maintenance. Instead she'd been spontaneous and fun.

Make-up and fashionable clothing might have been the order of the day when she was working, but when she was relaxing at home, or had any free time at all, she'd been at her happiest in jeans and T-shirts, and had kept the make-up to a bare minimum. Essentially she was an outdoors girl. Someone who loved the rain as much as the sunshine—who'd rather go for a hike in the countryside or a bicycle ride than saunter down the Kings Road in Chelsea and have every male in the vicinity turn to look at her. That was why Reece hadn't been able to understand her resistance to travelling with him in preference to staying at home.

But she was an emotional creature as well, and Sorrel's moods had had a significant bearing on her appetite. When she was upset or worried she barely touched her food. And that was Reece's main concern now. He simply *had* to convince her to maintain a healthy appetite—not just for her own sake but for the baby's too.

The baby… Returning the photograph carefully to the place where he had lifted it from, Reece scrubbed his hand round the stubble on his hard jaw with a sigh. *He was going to be a father.* That meant he had no choice but to lessen his working commitments over the next few months, and possibly for quite a while after the baby came. There was no way he wanted to be the kind of father who was away working practically the entire time his children were growing up—in spite of his reservations about whether the role would suit him or not. Something would have to be worked out that would benefit them all—him, Sorrel, and their child.

His career might have taken precedence over everything else up until now, but Reece knew it was time to take his foot off the gas a little where his ambition was concerned. It was time to learn to be something that he'd honestly never given much thought to before…a *family* man. Question was…could he do it for the baby's sake? Or was the rift between him and Sorrel simply too wide and too irretrievable for them to stand even the remotest chance of true happiness?

'Are you going to even attempt to eat that food, or are you simply just going to push it around your plate all night?'

Reece couldn't possibly be enjoying this agonising enforced togetherness in a smart restaurant beneath the eyes of its well-heeled patrons and attentive staff. And, as was evidenced by her singular lack of interest in the beautifully prepared linguine with asparagus, Sorrel herself certainly could not attest to enjoyment of any kind.

Frowning at her husband from the other side of the painstakingly laid table, with its white linen and shining silver-plated cutlery, she finally put down her fork and rested her hands wearily in her lap. 'I'm not hungry.'

'You're not hungry? Or you're deliberately being awkward just to spite me?' Throwing his napkin down beside his plate in disgust, Reece stared angrily back at her—his mouth a hard, admonishing line of disapproval and bitter disappointment.

So badly did Sorrel crave his forgiveness and kindness right then that she almost told him it was not so much because she wasn't hungry that she didn't eat—it was more because she was terrified of what food might do to her constantly unsettled stomach. He'd seen how it had been for her in the solicitor's office. Did he really want to witness such a dramatic and ungainly spectacle again, and this time in public?

'I told you we should have stayed home to eat,' was all she could bring herself to reply.

'I wanted us to come out to dinner and at least make an

effort towards establishing some kind of mutual understanding. The surroundings are pleasant, the food is first-class—all you had to do was sit back, relax and try to enjoy it. I might have known I was expecting too much.'

'It's not that I'm not—'

'Did you also forget that we had something special to celebrate?'

Raising his wine glass to his austere lips with deliberate irony, Reece took the smallest sip, then returned the glass to the table—the taste of the vintage Château Latour was clearly not delighting his palate in the way that fine wine usually did…not on *this* day anyway.

His deliberately provocative examination of Sorrel's slightly flushed features caused her blood to suddenly surge hotly, and in spite of her tension and unhappiness she couldn't resist the pull of the heat that radiated throughout her body. She might pretend that she was indifferent to his attention but it simply wasn't true. Judging by her spontaneous response just now she was as fervently attracted to Reece as ever.

'Do you really believe we have something special to celebrate? You've never even said how you felt about the baby.'

The memory sapped her confidence and filled her with doubt. He'd been purely practical from the start—bringing her home, buying her a pregnancy test, making plans to see the doctor when the result was positive. Everything except expressing what impact the news had had on him emotionally. Did he even really *want* this child? Sorrel knew how important Reece's career was to him. Did he perhaps fear that his new responsibilities as a father would encroach upon his absolute dedication to his work?

'Is that surprising, given the circumstances?'

He glanced away for a moment, as if having to contain his feelings in this most public arena was a constraint he'd rather not have to deal with right now.

'We never really discussed children, did we? I knew you were fond of your nephew and niece, but I assumed you'd want to wait at least a few more years down the line before having one of our own. You're only twenty-five, Sorrel. The last thing I ever wanted for you was you feeling tied down at becoming a mother at such a young age.'

'Why should having a baby make me feel tied down?' Her frown becoming even more pronounced, Sorrel pursed her pretty mouth, then chose her next words carefully, sudden optimism surfacing unexpectedly from somewhere deep inside her. 'We could still travel with you sometimes, couldn't we? Especially as the baby gets older? I wouldn't have to stay confined to the house all the time simply because I was a mother.'

'Funny, that. So you'd be willing to travel with me when the baby comes, yet before it's always been such a problem...like some kind of penance inflicted on you by virtue of being my wife?'

'What fun is it going sightseeing on my own while you're busy working, even if I might be in one of the most amazing places in the world? At least if I had the baby with me I'd have some company!'

Torn between frustration at her crazy logic and the unexpected humour that had sneaked up on him by surprise, Reece found himself leaning towards Sorrel and clasping her hand. Focusing on her beautiful, impassioned face, he could do nothing to halt the heated flow of blood that suddenly rushed into the lower half of his body and made every muscle exquisitely tense.

His appetite for food fled faster than when Reece was a boy, when he'd run and hide from his mother when she yelled at him to come and clean up his room. His appetite for wanting Sorrel to wrap her endlessly long slim legs around his lean hard middle and give him what he so badly yearned for became an obsession.

'We used to be so good together,' he reminded her, his tone lowered intimately as his hungry, examining gaze practically devoured her on the spot. 'What happened to us, Sorrel?'

For a tremulously long and arresting moment Sorrel allowed his destroyingly erotic green-eyed stare to seduce her. Her body—deprived of his love and affection for three tormenting months—inwardly preened itself like a cat stretched out beneath the healing soporific rays of a warm noonday sun. A hot, needy sensation surged into her nipples and made them long restlessly for his touch—his hands, his lips, and his heavenly taut-muscled chest as he pressed himself against her.

It was difficult to sit still as the powerfully erotic memory of what his touch could do to her took blatant hold. Unashamed carnal need pulsed between her thighs and Sorrel squeezed them tightly together to try and control her hungry, almost rapacious desire for her husband's attention there, too. The hurt and confusion that had kept her company for so long started inexorably to melt, and her lips started to edge helplessly towards a smile.

'It doesn't mean that things can't be good between us again just because there's a baby coming. You can't deny that you feel anything for me, Sorrel…I can see it in your eyes.'

Sorrel recaptured her smile in an instant as she assimilated Reece's words with ice-cold clarity. Her fears about him not really wanting the baby suddenly appeared distressingly correct, and all too dramatically any pleasure she might have found in anticipating his touch was ripped away—like a blissful dream that had suddenly and shockingly turned into a nightmare. She wrenched her hand deliberately free from his grasp.

'What do you mean "it doesn't mean that things can't be good between us again just because there's a baby coming"? You're against this pregnancy, aren't you? You don't want our child at all! I knew you didn't! Your only thought is to use the baby against me because *I* want it!' she snapped accusingly. Immediately she saw the heat and desire in Reece's eyes shockingly withdraw. In their place was an isolated wasteland that would make even the frozen outreaches of Alaska appear more like sunny Spain.

'Such a blatantly absurd lie doesn't even *deserve* a reply,' he told her scathingly, then signalled a nearby waiter for their bill.

The evening was spoiled before it had even really got started. Her heart throbbing hard inside her chest, Sorrel pushed to her feet. *Perhaps she shouldn't have come out with such a cruel accusation, but it was too late to take back the words now. And Reece still hadn't said anything to reassure her.* It was such a shame, when he'd been reaching out to her at last—showing her that he hadn't forgotten the hot sexual sparks that they'd generated so spontaneously between them.

In spite of her doubts, she couldn't help regretting her impulsive and unguarded behaviour. But with the ruins of her hopes and dreams silently devastating her, she started to walk away from their table. Reece immediately got to his feet and captured her arm. His touch had a distinct hint of steel in the fingers that wrapped around her slender-boned wrist, and for a moment Sorrel couldn't catch her breath.

'Where are you going?' he demanded, in a censorious undertone of barely contained fury.

'To the—to the ladies' washroom. Where do you *think* I'm going?'

He let her arm fall free with no lessening of the contempt in his glance. 'Don't be too long,' he instructed tersely. 'As soon as you get back we're leaving.'

It was a disaster. *They* were a disaster. Alone at the restaurant table, Reece took a longer slug of his wine and couldn't help wishing it were something far stronger. He'd give a lot right now to ease the almost unbearable tension that was painfully criss-crossing his midsection, making his whole body feel permanently bruised inside and out. It would be great to simply delude himself that there must be a way for him and Sorrel to find a way forward out of the mess they were in, but he seriously doubted it. However, if there wasn't…then God help their poor child.

But still…there was no way that Reece was just going to let Sorrel simply walk out on him again. More than ever she was *his* responsibility now, and he had a duty towards both her and the baby. If he did nothing else over the coming days and weeks he would get her to see that there was no getting away from that one immutable fact. They were *not* going to divorce and Sorrel was *not* going to cut him out of her life and remove both herself and their baby out of the sphere of his very necessary protection.

They were in this thing together and they would *stay* together—as one united family. *Nothing else would do…* Reece was absolutely resolved on that.

'Reece, *mi querido*! But how wonderful to see you!'

He glanced up in surprise at the confident ringing tones and the dark Latin beauty of the well-dressed woman in front of him. Angelina Cortez was a diva in every sense of the word. Reece had promoted nearly all of her concerts in the USA and Europe, and if her relentless demands had sometimes almost driven him crazy—well, he would forgive her every one the moment she opened her mouth to sing. The woman's exquisite voice could make the hardest heart melt at the emotion and passion that it emitted. The international acclaim she had attracted was more than deserved.

Rising to his feet, Reece kissed her affectionately on both cheeks, his senses momentarily hijacked by her seductive perfume and the dark flashing eyes that could no doubt have the same shocking effect as a stun gun on any healthy male who happened to be in the same vicinity.

'Angelina. You're looking more beautiful than ever, I see. What are you doing here in London? I thought you were taking a few months off to spend more time with little Emmanuel?'

'I am…I *have*! We have been travelling, my little son and I, and enjoying every minute of it! We flew in from Milan only yesterday…but what about you? Are you having dinner with a client, or is this a rare night off for you, *querido*? I've always said that you work too hard…even if it has been to my benefit!'

'I'm here with Sorrel…my wife.'

As he smiled into Angelina's interested eyes Reece glanced over her shoulder towards the other end of the restaurant, where Sorrel had disappeared in search of the ladies' washroom. He felt a twinge of concern that she was taking so long.

'You mean the delicate little blonde with the pretty blue eyes? You see—I remember! It would be charming to meet her properly and have dinner together some time, don't you think?'

'Yes, I'm sure Sorrel would enjoy that.'

He wasn't sure at all, but for politeness' sake he said it anyway.

'And in the meantime you and I must meet for lunch, Reece. I have been in talks with my agent this morning, and he wants me to do another American tour with perhaps one or two exclusive European dates thrown in. Of course you must promote me, as you did before. I will ring you in the next few days, OK? I am staying at the Dorchester, so I will book us a table there.'

Now wasn't the time to explain to Angelina that he would rather not take on such a big commitment with his wife being pregnant. But when they had lunch together, Reece would put her in the picture and give his regrets.

Feeling slightly on edge that Sorrel still hadn't returned, he loosened his collar a little and forced himself to smile at the ravishing star. 'I'll look forward to hearing from you.'

'*Adios, querido*. So lovely to see you again!'

* * *

Her feet inexorably slowing on the thick red carpet as she exited the Ladies', Sorrel watched in mute distress as she saw her husband embracing a stunningly beautiful brunette. Recognising the renowned opera star Angelina Cortez, she recalled the weeks and weeks Reece had spent away from home last year, travelling the world with the Spanish singer while she toured. The only contact she'd had during that interminable time they were apart had been Reece's daily telephone calls, and sometimes they'd only lasted a brief minute or two before he'd had to get back to giving all his attention to Angelina.

Had being apart from his wife been the hardship that it had been for Sorrel with *him* away? Somehow she didn't think so. Not when she rested her eyes on the beauty and elegance of the fascinating woman by his side. Jealousy and hurt immobilised her and made her knees feel decidedly shaky. Deliberately waiting until she saw Angelina move away from their table, Sorrel took her time walking back to join her husband.

'Is everything all right?'

Unable to hide the genuine concern that had made him so on edge at her absence, Reece studied her hard.

'Fine.'

Shrugging her shoulders, Sorrel picked up the black cashmere wrap that she'd left draped across her chair. 'Are you ready to leave now?'

'Can I get you anything?'

Pausing at the drinks cabinet, Reece undid his tie, shrugged off his jacket and threw them both on the back of a nearby couch. Sorrel had hardly spoken two words to him since they had left the restaurant. In spite of his vow that he would do everything he could to try and restore some harmony between them, he could barely hold back the rising tide of anger and resentment that was building inside him.

He would much rather deal with her temper than this cold, statue-like remoteness she was displaying towards him now. In her simple but elegant black dress, her pale moon-kissed limbs and light honey-blond hair made her look like a princess from a fairy tale who had been frozen in ice until the handsome prince came along and magically melted it away. In his heart Reece couldn't help wondering if he would be able to work any kind of magic at all on his lovely young wife to help restore her affections towards him.

'No, thanks. I think I'll just go straight to bed.'

'Alone?'

His green eyes alighting with a speculative glitter upon her startled face, Reece struggled with his growing irritation at her deliberate withdrawal of contact.

'I'm not ready to—I mean for us to share a bedroom just yet. Please understand.'

There was genuine pain in her soft, bewitching voice, and for a moment Reece's anger relented, even though her reluctance to have him back in her bed cut him to the quick.

'Go on. Go to bed, Sorrel. I'll see you in the morning.'

Turning back to the drinks cabinet, Reece poured himself a generous measure of the Scotch he'd been craving at dinner and took a slug. As the familiar burn slid down into his stomach, he realised he had never felt so low…not even when Sorrel had walked out on him. It was damn hard to go through the motions of living when every little bit of spark inside him had been inexorably extinguished by the slow but deadening deterioration of his relationship with his wife.

'Was that Angelina Cortez I saw you talking to in the restaurant tonight?' Sorrel asked him from behind.

Nursing his glass of Scotch, Reece processed the question with a spurt of surprise and did an about-turn. His expression was instantly wary.

'You saw us? Why didn't you come and say hello?'

With a flush of guilt, Sorrel glanced quickly away from the censure in his compelling eyes.

'The two of you seemed quite happy together without me joining in,' she replied, forcing her tone to sound deliberately airy. 'Is she going to be touring again soon?'

Knowing he shouldn't be so stunned by her astuteness, Reece imbibed another generous gulp of whisky before replying. 'Maybe. Why do you want to know?'

Hugging the warm cashmere wrap more tightly across her chest, Sorrel could not hide her sharp disappointment and fear. 'Obviously I'll need to know if you're going to be away for months on end again…especially now that the baby's coming.'

'Of course, I'll be taking that into account.'

He didn't want to go into detail right now. Instinctively he knew that if he did Sorrel would only read any explanation he might offer in the wrong way. Her hostility was as inevitable as the tides, it seemed.

'She's a widow, isn't she? She must like having you

dance attention on her hand and foot when you're away together.'

Even though common sense loudly dictated that she didn't push this any further than she ought, her sorrow at losing her husband's affection made Sorrel dice with death. Her heart started to throb deeply as she waited for his inevitable cutting comment.

With a look of harsh dismay, Reece curled his mouth disparagingly at the corner. 'I don't "dance attention" on her, for God's sake! I promote the woman's concerts—that's all...period! If you acted more like a real wife and travelled with me when I work you'd see the truth for yourself!'

His acid statement burning her inside, Sorrel blindly reached for the catch on the door and fled out into the corridor.

CHAPTER FOUR

IN HER dream Reece and Angelina Cortez were laughing at her—holding hands and mocking her misery as she anguished and wept and felt as if she was being flayed alive by a whip studded with red-hot nails.

'You don't know how to be a *real* wife!' Reece taunted her, his mouth twisted and his eyes hard as flint.

'Yes, I do!' Sorrel cried, over and over, the pain jack-knifing through her middle as though her very flesh was being sliced open. 'Please give me another chance, Reece! I promise I'll try and be the wife you want!'

Her deep sorrow—along with a very real excruciating pain low down in her stomach—woke her up. Her brow was slippery with perspiration and her short cotton nightgown was uncomfortably damp. As she forced herself to sit up, acute waves of debilitating pain almost made her head fall back onto the pillow again. So intensely sharp were they that it was all she could do to gulp down enough air to breathe.

Her distress increased dramatically when she threw back the sheet and satin counterpane and saw to her avid horror that her white nightgown was stained not with perspiration but with *blood*. Immediately Sorrel started to shake, her hands clutching her stomach, and she was keening, 'Oh, God, oh, God…' as she realised with stark cold terror that she must be losing the baby.

Knowing that if he was deep in the middle of sleep—in his room several yards down the hall from hers—Reece was not likely to hear her shouts of distress, Sorrel had no choice but to force herself to her feet and try and get to the door. With her nightgown pressed tight between her legs, terrified by the stream of blood that seemed to be gushing down her pale, slender thighs as though it would never stop, she managed to hobble to the door and wrench it open.

'Reece!' she cried out in rising hysteria as she held onto the door with one hand and her nightgown with the other, her fear escalating almost out of control as she struggled to deal with the horror of it all. 'Oh, God…Reece—help me, please!'

He had been dreaming too…dark, disturbing, haunting dreams that made him break out in an icy cold sweat. When Sorrel's sudden shout of distress pierced his subconscious, Reece moved like lightning up into a sitting position, his heart thudding so acutely that it immediately alerted him to danger.

Orientating himself, he frantically wondered if he had imagined the whole thing or whether it had just been part of the general nightmare he'd been disturbed by. When he heard Sorrel's voice for real—genuine distress turning into a frightened, almost childlike sob—he threw his legs out of the bed, flung out through the door dressed only in a pair of blue cotton pyjama bottoms, and came face to face with the kind of horrific scene he wouldn't wish on his worst enemy.

All he could see at first was the blood. There was so much of it, and his rapidly wakening brain tried to make sense of the dreadful sight with its usually insistent logic—telling him that she must have tripped and fallen somehow, and badly cut herself. At that precise moment Reece couldn't allow himself to believe that the shocking scarlet stains defiling his wife's virginal white nightgown were anything to do with the baby. *Their* baby. The child that Reece had fathered. His son or daughter. *Please God, no…*

'What's wrong, honey? What have you done to yourself? Tell me, Sorrel…let me help you!'

He tried to lead her back into the bedroom, but she suddenly bent over doubled up in agony, her hand a white-knuckled clamp around the hard edge of the door. From this angle all Reece could see was the top of her ravishing blond hair and the smooth buttermilk skin of her neck, where the impossibly delicate silken curls fell away. But then his gaze locked in dread onto the pool of blood that was trickling down through her toes and staining the cream rug she was standing on. It was clear then that his fears about the baby were more than real. *Sorrel was losing it…*

His throat locked tight as emotion overwhelmed him. But then Sorrel cried out again, and Reece knew he had to get her to the hospital before she bled to death. That one goal in mind, he swung her up into his arms and carried her to the bed. As she lay there, frightened and sobbing, he held onto her hands, wishing they weren't so cold, and looked urgently into her terrified blue eyes.

'Sweetheart, I'm going to have to get you to the hospital. I'm not going to phone for an ambulance because I can get you there quicker myself. It's going to be all right, angel…I promise. Just let me wrap this around you to keep you warm, and we'll get going.'

Pulling the aubergine-coloured counterpane from the bed, Reece placed it tenderly around Sorrel's shoulders, lightly touched her face, then lifted her up again into his arms.

'Am I going to die, Reece?' she asked him, her voice quivering. 'There's so much bl-blood!'

There was no point in asking him if she was going to lose the baby. She'd known as soon as she'd woken up with that terrible knifing pain practically slicing her middle in two and seen the vivid scarlet stains on her gown that that was practically a certainty.

She felt Reece's strong arms enfolding her even more tightly, the muscles in his biceps bunching like iron. His gaze was reassuringly fierce as he stared back at her. 'You are not going to die, Sorrel…don't you dare even think about it! We're going to get you to the hospital and everything's going to be just fine…do you hear me?'

Her eyes were drifting closed as another wave of pain stole away the words she'd been going to say, but one clear thought rang out in her mind above all the rest. *Reece was wrong…delusional or just too ridiculously optimistic for words…* Because after this nothing was going to be fine ever again. Even in her traumatised state of mind Sorrel already knew that.

* * *

The ceiling was very white and clinical, and as Sorrel stared up at it, her mind determinedly trying not to focus on the terror and pain she had just survived, she bizarrely recalled a similar ceiling in her dentist's surgery. As pale and clinical as this one, it was nonetheless transformed by a wonderful colour poster of a sun-drenched Caribbean island. The scene comprised a sweeping crystalline sandy beach and swaying palm trees, and on the horizon miles and miles of iridescent ocean, sparkling off into the distance.

That poster never failed to transport her to another world. While the dentist attended to her teeth Sorrel would determinedly concentrate her gaze upon it until he'd finished treating her. And as she dreamed about lying on that sublime beach and inhaling the evocative scents of coconut and sea breezes, feeling the kiss of that Caribbean sun on her skin, she barely even noticed the time passing in the dentist's chair. *She wished she could call upon her ability to dream the time away now, and be the fresh-faced eager young girl again, that Reece had fallen head-over-heels in love with.* But how could she when her heart felt as though a rusty three-inch nail had been driven into it with force and her soul felt shrivelled and all used up?

Experiencing a powerful urge to cry, Sorrel couldn't give vent to her need—because the strong sedation she had been given acted like an impenetrable stone wall between her heart and her tears and they simply would not come. Biting down hard on her parched lips instead, she deliberately shut her eyes, truly feeling that the darkness was somehow much more preferable to the light right now….

* * *

He felt like a survivor of a train wreck, or something equally shocking. Staring into the mirror above the chipped enamel sink in the men's room at the hospital, Reece hardly recognised himself. Every feature on his face was tinged with the shadow of heartbreak and the horror of his enforced descent into darkness when he had realised that not only was Sorrel losing their baby, but she might just possibly lose her life, too.

He'd sensed the medical team's urgency as they'd shut him out of the operating theatre, and again and again Reece's heart had slammed against his ribs as he waited for the surgeon in charge to reappear. *By the time he'd got Sorrel to the hospital she'd lost so much blood.* He'd had a nightmare journey to get her there—not because of traffic, but because her cries of pain and distress had torn him apart inch by torturous inch. *And it was all his fault.* If he hadn't made her come out to dinner when she was clearly not feeling up to it… If he hadn't rowed with her and threatened her with court proceedings if she didn't come home with him… If he had only tried to be more understanding about this desire of hers for him to be home with her more often rather than away travelling for most of the time…

As he stared into that cold, unflattering square of cracked and tired mirror Reece reflected in silent agony on all the things he could possibly have done to make his wife feel more loved. He hadn't wept tears since he was fourteen, when they had told him that his mother was dying and wouldn't survive the cancer that had eventually taken her away from him. He'd gone to stay with his aunt

Shirley in New York and had locked all his feelings away deep inside him, in the hope that he could barricade his wounded heart against any such devastating hurt again.

In the past few hours Reece had discovered that his heart was just as vulnerable than ever. If not more. Now he wanted to weep and never stop. Tears pricked his eyelids like taunting spearmen pushing him towards the edge of a cliff. But as his sight became suddenly blurred by the threatened deluge he turned away in disgust and shame and pushed out through the door into the long medicinal-smelling corridor of the hospital where he had brought Sorrel. Almost as soon as he did so, he mentally started to steel himself to come face to face with her after the trauma of last night, and couldn't help fearing that he was woefully inadequate to the task.

She had her hands curled into fists beside her on the sheet and her lovely face was as pale as a winter moon as Reece approached the bed. Silently thanking God that they'd taken down the drip they'd put up last night, and that she was free from tubes and wires and all the frightening hospital equipment that denoted a critical condition, he felt the smallest release of tension ease out between his shoulder blades.

There was a hard grey vinyl chair beside the bed, but apart from the plain yellowed locker at the other side of Sorrel the room was pretty much bare of any decoration or comfort. *Stark* was perhaps the word he would use to describe it. He would get her out of here just as soon he got the all-clear from the surgeon, he quickly decided. She couldn't possibly recuperate in such a depressing environment. But all the same he was grateful for everything the medical team had done. They had saved his wife's life and given her the privacy of a room of her own for the first day at least. He hadn't particularly relished the idea of speaking to Sorrel for the first time since the traumatic events of last night in a ward filled with other patients.

Turning to regard him, Sorrel registered his presence with her eyes, like a sleepwalker suddenly stumbling awake—and the brief streak of fear and anxiety reflected in the grief-stricken blue depths made Reece's stomach contract in pain, as though his bare flesh had suddenly been penetrated by a sharp blade.

'Hello,' she said softly, the unexpectedly husky quality of her gentle voice sending shivers cascading down Reece's spine.

Reaching for her clenched fist, he stroked across her knuckles with the pad of his thumb…back and forth, back and forth. She reacted by uncurling her fingers a little, like a nervous bud cautious about flowering. Even after the shocking events she had been through she was still the most ravishing creature Reece had ever laid eyes on. Her pale, delicate, and yet at the same time striking features were poignantly bare of any artifice save her own natural beauty, and although he wasn't blind to the pale mauve shadows beneath her eyes, or the sorrowful downturn of her mouth, her loveliness still shone through the pain.

He wanted badly to kiss her. He desired it so much that he almost trembled with his need to feel that wondrously tender skin beneath his own. But fear of rejection was an ever-present companion to that need, so Reece held back—praying for a sign—the smallest, most fleeting indication from Sorrel—that she might welcome his kiss.

'Hi.' He smiled down at her, behind the tenderly bestowed gesture wondering if he would see *her* sweet lips curve into a smile of joy or happiness in his presence ever again. 'How are you doing?'

'I hurt.'

Reece flinched. 'I know you do, honey, and I wish I could take all the pain away for you—God help me, I do. You were so brave, sweetheart…brave and strong. As soon as I've seen your doctor I'm getting you out of here to somewhere much nicer, so that you can be more comfortable.'

His face was bereft of colour, his strongly delineated features almost stark with shock and sorrow. As she studied him, Sorrel registered a fresh wave of pain that was nothing to do with her physical hurts. He might have smiled at her, but behind that smile was an ocean of suppressed agony that she couldn't deny. It was there in the sombre set of his jaw, in the dark circles beneath the now dulled emerald of his fascinating eyes and the tiny, deeply indented grooves bracketing his mouth.

Reece had clearly had to reach deep down inside himself to even find the will to make that smile. Yet part of Sorrel couldn't help fretting—was he privately *relieved* that she had lost the baby? She knew it was a terrible, probably totally undeserved judgement, yet the undeniable pressure of it threatened to seriously impede her breathing. *Now there would be no need for him to change or alter his commitment to work in any way.* For Reece, things could return to normal. For Sorrel, *dying* seemed like the only acceptable alternative right now.

'Do I have to move?' she asked, frowning. 'I'm OK here.'

Her eyes spoke volumes to Reece of her need to deny herself comfort of any kind, and the realisation disturbed him deeply.

'You mustn't blame yourself for what happened, Sorrel. How can any of us know why it did? Maybe your body just wasn't ready to cope with pregnancy? What you need now is the best of care and lots of rest to help you recover. Then, when you're strong again, I'll take you somewhere warm and beautiful. We'll go away for a couple of months maybe? Take our time, get to know each other all over again.'

'Forget about the baby, you mean? Pretend that this never happened?'

'I didn't say that!'

'We should have gone through with the divorce proceedings, Reece. We should have just followed through and had done with it. You didn't want the baby. You didn't really want *me*. You were only mad at me because I left and took matters into my own hands. The most important thing to you has always been your career. Rubbing shoulders with people like Angelina Cortez…that's all you've ever really wanted, Reece. Not a wife and baby…no way.'

Sorrel was almost incoherent with grief. One thought bumped against another, just giving way to a flood of rage and hurt that pained her worse than the dreadful killing ache deep inside her womb.

Someone ought to pay for the terrible thing that had happened to her. Sorrel's greatest hope for them both had been that they could create a strong, secure, loving family—just like her own had been. *Why was that so hard for her to achieve with Reece?* Because ultimately he was *wrong* for her, she decided, tearing her glance away from the astounded expression on his face. Losing the baby was surely a sign that this man she had chosen was *wrong* for her.

'You think that this doesn't hurt me as much as it hurts you, Sorrel?' His voice threatening to break with grief, Reece willed his wife to look at him. Slowly, reluctantly, she lifted her gaze to regard him.

'Just yesterday I learnt that I was going to be a father. Yes, the news came as a shock—I won't lie to you about that.' A tiny muscle flinched beneath his eye. 'Now…only a day later…that realisation has been ripped away from me in the most terrible way. Do you think that I'm made of stone? I'm devastated by what's happened to you…to *us*.'

Shaking his golden-haired head in anguished silence, Reece moved restlessly away from the bed. 'I *wanted* our baby, Sorrel. I wanted this chance to be a better husband to you and a good father to our child. Now it seems that I've lost both those chances. If you think that my career is the most important thing to me at a time like this then you couldn't be more wrong. And I'm not going to simply let you wallow in your own grief and feel that you're in this nightmare on your own. I'll be here for you every step of the way…you can count on it.'

His mouth softening a little round the edges, Reece walked right back up to the bed and studied her tenderly. 'As dreadful as you're feeling now…I promise you that things will get better, sweetheart. I'm in this marriage for better or worse, and nothing's going to change my mind about that. Am I getting through to you, Sorrel?'

'Mrs Villiers…how are you feeling this morning?'

They were both saved from further heartbreaking interaction as the surgeon who had looked after Sorrel last night walked into the room, accompanied by another doctor and a nurse. And as Reece reluctantly tore his gaze away from his wife's troubled blue-eyed glance, he knew he was absolutely determined to follow through with everything he had said to her.

A week later, and home again, it came as a deep shock to Sorrel to realise that even though she had lost her baby she still felt as if she was pregnant. They'd told her at the hospital where she'd gone to recuperate that it would take a while for her hormones to settle down again and return to normal, and that she wasn't to worry. But the after-effects of her miscarriage only served to remind her that her body was no longer preparing to carry her baby to term, that all the sickness and lethargy and bouts of crying she'd suffered had all been for nothing.

What was making things worse was Reece's unexpected presence in the house. He might have told Sorrel in no uncertain terms that he fully intended to stay in this marriage for 'better or worse', but she really hadn't expected him to take so much time off work simply just to be with her. She knew the situation was unprecedented, but even so Reece had never sacrificed his desire to immerse himself in his work before. The fact that they were barely talking to each other—mainly because Sorrel deliberately withdrew into silence whenever he walked into the same room as her—didn't seem to bother Reece that much. He simply asked her if she needed anything, closed the window against any draughts, brought her magazines, a sandwich, an occasional cup of tea or coffee, and then left her alone with her thoughts with the proviso that if she did need anything else she was to tell him immediately.

Sorrel speculated on how long they could continue in such an emotionally sterile state. She was beginning to think that she preferred the jagged heat of their many arguments rather than the suffocating fog of silence that had descended on them both. Any day now she fully expected Reece to walk in and tell her that he'd had enough of playing nursemaid and that he was returning to work. Knowing that she was nowhere near getting over the loss of her baby, Sorrel wouldn't have blamed him. It must be like living with a lifeless marble statue instead of a living, breathing woman.

'Want to go out for a while?'

His slow and deep, almost gravelly voice broke into her thoughts, and for a moment the rich warm tones caused a throb of heat to flare somewhere deep inside her. *Sorrel had always loved Reece's voice.* It stroked over her nerve endings with the combined seductive heat of the most desired French brandy and rich dark velvet and made her long to lean into his arms and just simply give way to the security and warmth of the strength that she knew she would find there. *How good would it be to stop grieving alone and simply reach out to each other again like they used to?*

Dropping the edge of the curtain she'd pulled back to glance out of the window, she glanced back at him in surprise.

'Where?' She shrugged, her heart helplessly lifting at the sight of his tall straight physique, silently admiring the way his stylish black jeans and grey lambswool sweater complemented his lean, yet nicely muscled body. Sorrel noticed too the chestnut lights glinting in his dark gold hair, and the way one corner of his delicious mouth was almost curving into a smile. Her resistance started to seriously be compromised.

'I thought we could take a walk in Kensington Gardens…just a short one—nothing too taxing. Are you up for that?'

She had barely eaten a thing since her return from hospital, and as Reece's probing gaze swept his wife's almost too slender form in her cream-coloured cardigan and brown linen skirt, he was alarmed to discover that she appeared to have lost even more weight. His heart pounded against ribs that already felt contused by anguish and grief.

'OK. I'm going stir-crazy just staying in the house anyway.'

Her agreement at going for a walk totally took Reece by surprise. As soon as he'd made the suggestion he'd fully expected her to say no, and he'd been steeling himself against it. Now a flicker of hope started to throb inside him.

'It might be a good idea to put on some jeans and boots. It's been raining off and on all morning, and there's probably a good deal of mud around.'

'OK.'

Curling some soft blond tendrils behind her ear, Sorrel almost offered him a smile…*almost…but not quite*. As Reece followed her progress out of the room, he let loose the deeply weary sigh he'd been holding onto practically the whole week and sank down into a nearby red leather armchair to get his bearings.

CHAPTER FIVE

'WHEN were you intending going back to work?'

Her gaze focused on the large stretch of water before them known as the Serpentine—where ducks, geese and swans congregated in busy little groups intent on getting their share of the bread that children were happily throwing out to them—Sorrel dug her hands deep into the pockets of her green puffa jacket and tried to stem the tide of melancholy that washed over her. Today there was no discernible sunshine, because the sun was hiding shy behind a bank of stormy-looking grey clouds, and it perfectly echoed the lack of any kind of brightness in her heart.

They both came to a standstill, staring out at the lake in unison, the chattering of children and birds alike flowing over them, silently grating on the unseen bruises of their shared heartbreak. Reece lifted a shoulder and only glanced at his wife briefly, as if the sight of her sadness these days was almost too much for even his broad shoulders to bear.

'I'm not in any rush to get back to work, Sorrel. I have other people to help take care of things in my absence…you know that. I'll take as much time out as you need.'

She didn't deviate from her intense perusal of the lake. She just stared as if both she and her thoughts were miles away.

'That's the whole point, Reece. I don't "need" you to take any more time off work to be with me. What purpose is it serving? I'm miserable, you're miserable—how is it helping either of us? At least if you got back to work you could focus on something else instead of this—this.' Sorrel had been going to use the word 'hell', but withdrew it at the last second as her womb contracted with a sudden piercing ache deep inside her.

One day all this would be behind her. One day the pain she was experiencing now would not be so brutal—so raw—making her feel like she wanted to escape her own skin just to get some relief. If she didn't believe that her agony would diminish, even a little, she might as well just lie down and die right now. There had to be the promise of a day in the not too far distant future when her life would return to normal again, when she could start to come to terms with the fact that once upon a time all her hopes and dreams had been ripped away from her—like a boat torn from its moorings by a freak storm that had occurred out of the blue.

'We're in this together, Sorrel. I told you that before. Why should I want to focus on anything else but us?'

'You didn't want the baby.'

'For God's sake, don't keep saying that!'

Agony piercing him at her cruel assertion, Reece curled his hands into fists down by his sides and clenched his jaw.

It took him several seconds to put out the fire of anger that arose inside him, but he couldn't extinguish it completely. It stayed simmering beneath the surface even as he told himself it was only his wife's deep misery about the loss of the baby she'd carried that made her say such blatantly untrue things. She needed to lash out at somebody over the unfairness of it all. It hadn't helped their case that their relationship had been at its lowest ebb when she'd discovered she was pregnant. And because of that, she naturally wanted to blame Reece for everything.

'Anyway…I think you should go back to work. I've got things I need to concentrate on myself.'

Her blue eyes settled on him a little nervously, Reece thought—as though she were unsure of her ground since his outburst of temper. If only he could find the words to reassure her, to tell her that he would never willingly cause her any more pain in a million years. But right then—with the voices of excited young children ringing out in the chilly spring day—Reece's ability to think with any real clarity just got wrapped up in the innocent yet hurtful sounds, and he bent down, picked up a pebble and threw it into the water so that it skimmed across the dull, slightly green surface and made three distinct splashes as it progressed out into the centre of the lake.

'What "things" do you need to concentrate on?' he asked.

'I want to get back to work myself. Not modelling,' she added quickly as she registered Reece's swift frown of disapproval. 'I've been working on some fashion designs, and Nina Bryant thinks that they're really quite good. I know a lot of people in the business still, and I think I could make a go of something if I give it my all.'

Reece hated to burst her bubble, he really did, but in his opinion no way was Sorrel ready to throw herself into another career—let alone 'give it her all.' She hadn't given herself proper time either to grieve or heal, and if this fashion designing didn't work out the disappointment could set her back even further. Much more pressing was the need for them both to try and repair the damage that had been done to their marriage, so that they could weather this new storm together with some strength.

'I don't think now is the time to be thinking about starting out in something else, Sorrel.' His frown deepened, furrowing the lightly tanned skin on his forehead. 'I think we should go away somewhere, like I suggested before. We could go to the house in the Algarve. At this time of year it won't be too hot, and we can just spend time together and relax.'

'I don't want any more time to relax or think or brood! Can't you see that? I need to keep myself occupied. I really don't want to go away on holiday, Reece. Don't you think I would go out to Australia if I wanted to, and stay with my parents if I needed a break? My mum and dad have already asked me.' But Sorrel hadn't felt able to face her beloved parents' distress about the loss of her baby and deal with her own as well—*or* capitulate to her sister Melody's insistence that she return to Suffolk and stay with her. Best to steer clear of other people expressing their emotions right now, when she wasn't exactly feeling strong or prepared.

'And what about us?'

Reece turned to face her head-on and Sorrel caught the merest glimpse of a muscle flexing slightly in the plane of his beautiful angled cheekbone. She sensed the undoubted tension building inexorably inside him, as though he was on a very short fuse that was going to ignite any second now.

'Us?'

'Don't you think it would do us both good to get away together? To have time to rest and relax and make some decisions about our future?'

Her heart jumped. *Hadn't he already told her he was in this 'for better or worse'? Was he now changing his mind?*

'I'll still agree to a divorce, if that's what you want.'

Inside, Sorrel was so frozen she felt as if she'd been buried beneath an icy avalanche that she would never escape from.

'There's not going to be any divorce. I told you that already! Instead I'm going to be right beside you while you heal, and we're going to work things out together—as we should have done right from the beginning, when everything started to fall apart. Do you hear me?'

She flinched at his uncompromisingly irritated tone, and at the perfectly delineated features that were so compelling. All she ever seemed to do these days was make him furious with her. But there were no manuals available with 'quick fixes' in them, to tell her how to get over this terrible thing that had happened to her and stop destroying the one thing that she'd always counted on until recently…*her husband's love.*

Turning away from the sight of the lake and the activity surrounding it, Sorrel returned her chilled hands to her pockets and started to walk away.

'Sorrel!'

Reece chased after her, halting her progress with the ring of command that inevitably laced his voice. Studying him with dulled blue eyes, Sorrel wished that the day, her body, and her life didn't all feel so deathly, irredeemably cold.

'I'm sorry,' he ground out, the cold air turning his breath to steam. 'I'm not trying to upset you. I'm merely trying to get you to see that I want to help you. I've never seen you so low…do you know what that does to me?'

'It's OK.' Grimacing slightly, Sorrel could hardly bring herself to meet his eyes. 'You probably deserve a much better wife than me, Reece.'

'Don't say that!'

'I've brought you nothing but trouble.'

'Why are you doing this, Sorrel? Isn't it enough that we've both suffered over what's happened without punishing ourselves even more?' Wanting to ease her anxiety and let her feel his genuine support, Reece reached out and brushed a lock of her hair tenderly away from her eyebrow. 'Why don't you let me make an appointment with a doctor or a bereavement counsellor to get you some help?'

Could some cool, detached professional help show her the way out of her sorrow and pain? The idea didn't fill her with much reassurance. Swallowing down a fresh wave of despair, Sorrel glanced up into Reece's warm, concerned gaze.

'I know that you mean well, but I'm not ready to talk about this with anyone else just yet.'

'That's OK, honey.' He touched her mouth, then withdrew his hand with a smile. 'When you're ready, we'll get you all the help that you need. In the meantime I'm here for you—twenty-four seven…you got that?'

Because he was smiling at her, Sorrel couldn't resist the warmth that the gesture engendered in all the icy little corners of her heart. Her hand moved towards him and she found her fingers curling tentatively around his. Registering his surprise and pleasure, she allowed her grip to tighten a little. 'Can we walk a little more, do you think?'

'Of course…as long as you don't overdo things.'

Feeling his heart lift for the first time in days, Reece remembered what sweet pleasure it was just to do something as simple and innocent as hold hands with his beautiful wife….

Despite their fledgling truce at the park, they were still sleeping in separate rooms, with Sorrel continuing to fight shy of making conversation and withdrawing into herself for hours on end.

When the telephone rang on his study desk one evening about a week later, Reece was actually genuinely pleased to hear the exotic Spanish tones of the beautiful Angelina Cortez.

'Reece, *mi querido!* I rang your office but they told me that you were on leave. I am so glad to find you at home! I was hoping we could still have lunch together, as I suggested before? Would tomorrow at one o'clock suit? I am still at the Dorchester, so we can eat there. Please say that you can join me?'

Knowing that Sorrel had already turned down his suggestion of lunch tomorrow at one of the new Conran restaurants in town, Reece rubbed his hand round the back of his neck to ease the strain that had accumulated there from the past few weeks and quickly scribbled the time down in his opened diary.

'One o'clock will be just fine, Angelina. I'll look forward to seeing you tomorrow.'

'And I have to ask…have you thought any more about accepting my offer to organise a new tour for me? I am anxious to know.'

Ordinarily Reece would think *Why not?* and relish the prospect—although challenging, with a star like Angelina—of getting his teeth into another demanding and all-consuming project. But right now there was no enthusiastic response left in him—not when all he could think about was Sorrel, and when and if she would ever show even the merest glimpse of returning to a normal life again. Because his emotions were so affected by his wife's melancholic moods, he questioned his own ability even to pull off a major project like the American tour Angelina had in mind.

'We'll talk about it tomorrow, if you don't mind,' was all he said, and at Angelina's subdued *adios* he put down the receiver.

Pausing outside the door of her husband's modern and spacious study, Sorrel let her hand drop to her side instead of knocking to go in, and drew her finely arched brows together in a helpless expression of anguish. *Reece was going to meet Angelina Cortez for lunch tomorrow.*

What was the 'it' they were going to talk about? Sorrel longed to know. Since losing the baby her anxiety about her relationship with Reece had become even more acute. She ached to discuss her feelings with him, to ask him to give her time and not become despondent that she was so uncommunicative and withdrawn—and *especially* not to seek comfort in the arms of someone else. Someone vital and exotic and lovely…like Angelina Cortez… But how could she even begin when she knew in her heart that he had to be getting tired of her behaviour?

It had been months now since they had had any kind of intimate relations, and there would be another month yet—the gynaecologist at the hospital had told her—before 'normal' sexual activity could resume. It didn't help Sorrel that she was terrified of resuming *any* kind of intimacy with her angry and frustrated husband. They had both levelled some terrible accusations at each other, and how did they go about healing the scars of all that? How could Sorrel start to see herself as a desirable woman again when her body wouldn't even allow her to carry a baby to full term?

The door opened suddenly while she was standing there thinking, and she jumped back in surprise. Reece's commanding frame stilled in the doorway, and his glance was wary, as if he wondered what new problem his wife was going to present him with now. It hardly reassured Sorrel to imagine that her own husband viewed her as someone with an endless list of problems and demands.

'What is it?' he asked.

'I—I think I might like to go out to lunch tomorrow after all.'

Finding it hard to meet the searing examination of his forthright gaze, Sorrel glanced down at her unpainted nails and pushed back the cuticle of her forefinger with the nail of her thumb. She knew perfectly well that Reece was meeting Angelina tomorrow, and she wanted to know what he would do about it if she presented him with this new dilemma. Would he choose the sultry opera star over his sad, depressed wife?

'What made you change your mind?'

'I—I…' Shrugging a shoulder, Sorrel found she couldn't lie. Lies would only dig them both into a deeper and deeper slough of despond. 'I heard you on the phone just now. You're meeting Angelina Cortez, aren't you?'

'Dammit, Sorrel! Just what the hell do you think you're playing at? Have things got so bad that you have to resort to hanging around outside my study door listening to my phone calls?'

'I only heard by accident,' she protested, her blue eyes revealing her hurt that he believed she would deliberately do a thing like that.

'So if you know I've already agreed to meet Angelina why are you now telling me *you* want to go to lunch after all?'

'Is it a business lunch?'

Sorrel had to know, because her very bones ached at the thought that it might be something more.

Disappointment, pain and sheer disbelief briefly clouded Reece's enigmatic features.

'Of *course* it's a business lunch! What are you suggesting, Sorrel? That I'm having an affair with the woman?'

Her mouth went dry as chalk. 'Are you?' Her lips quivered a little and she drew her hand across her ribcage beneath her sweater, to try and quell the churning that was going on inside.

'No. I'm *not* having an affair.'

Leaning a shoulder against the doorjamb, Reece didn't bother to hide his weariness. All of a sudden Sorrel pined for him to hold her. She wanted to bury her face in his broad, hard chest so badly. She knew a great need to smell the heavenly, rather exotic tang of the aftershave cologne he used, which would be mingled with his own innately gorgeous smell. She wanted to feel him slide his fingers through the soft strands of her long blond hair and then raise her face to his for a deep and satisfying kiss. A kiss that would reassure her that he still loved her. *Oh, how she craved all those things!*

But as she continued to regard him she saw him mentally withdraw from her rather than share her need to be closer. If only she could just find it in herself to tell him that she was sorry for everything—that she knew she had played her part in helping them drift further and further apart—that he wasn't solely to blame. Longing to share with him her grief about the baby, she also wanted to confess that she'd *always* had a secret desire to bear his child. But, knowing instinctively that children had never been a particular desire for him, as they'd been for her, Sorrel had held back from admitting it in case he told her to her face that he absolutely did not want children—period. She'd been far too scared to hear him say the words she'd dreaded.

But how was she supposed to tell him all those things now when she didn't even know if he really loved her any more? Only a couple of weeks ago he'd been going to divorce her, and he'd only withdrawn from that intention when he'd learned that Sorrel might be pregnant.

'So Angelina is thinking of touring again, is she?'

Trying to make her tone conversational, Sorrel crossed her restless arms in front of her chest.

Straightening up from where he'd been leaning against the door, Reece nodded once, as if silently confirming something to himself.

'You're not interested in my work, Sorrel. You never have been. So don't start pretending now. If you really want to go to lunch tomorrow I'll cancel my meeting with Angelina. Of course I will. But if you're only saying that you want to go because you've got some dumb idea that I'm having an affair…then forget it. I'll be working late tonight, so go to bed whenever you're ready. I'll see you in the morning.'

Withdrawing into the room behind him, he didn't hesitate to shut the door in her face.

Getting up for a glass of water and some headache pills at three in the morning, Sorrel crossed the tiled kitchen floor in her bare feet, her silk robe flapping open across her matching short silk nightgown as she headed towards the sink.

Her headache had developed, she was convinced, because her mind was just so restless with thinking. Past, present and future were all melding into one hazy blur, pressing on her tired brain—the happiness of the distant past sadly and heavily outweighed by the unhappiness of the present and Sorrel's dread of the future.

Filling a tumbler with some cold water at the tap, she stood still, her mind gravitating to their house in the Algarve, Portugal—a place Reece had owned long before he'd met Sorrel and that he'd had redecorated to her taste just after they'd married. It was a very gracious old building that used to be a farmhouse, and Reece had had some very exclusive and innovative designers flown in especially from Italy to redesign the interiors.

Sorrel recalled the steamy and very satisfying three weeks that she and Reece had spent there the summer before last. They'd hardly left their bed, other than to eat or bathe or wander around the local charming little streets of the nearest town holding hands and delighting in anything and everything that met their eyes. They had been so in love and happy. Why—only just over a year later on into their marriage—had that feeling somehow drifted away from them?

'I thought I heard a noise down here. Is everything all right?'

Startled, Sorrel spun round to see Reece enter the room. He was bare to the waist, adorned only in black silk pyjama bottoms that settled low on his tanned lean hips, exposing his navel and, further up, a light column of fine blond hair dusting across a sublimely masculine chest that was proportioned just perfectly. *Sorrel had almost forgotten just how beautifully he was made.* She just stared at him…she couldn't help it. It would have been like asking a child not to notice the sweets at the checkout in a supermarket.

'I only wanted some headache pills.'

'Oh?'

The concern that flashed across Reece's face was deep and immediate. He walked towards her with that slow, unconsciously sexy gait of his that stole all the breath from her lungs and started a sensuous ache deep and low in her belly.

Not many women could look as heavenly as she did woken from sleep in the middle of the night. Even when she was old his wife would remain a truly classic beauty, Reece speculated to himself as he watched her. With her face wiped clean of any trace of make-up, her eyes drowsy from sleep and her blond hair sexily tousled from where she'd lain her head on the pillow, his lovely young wife was the kind of bewitching sight that any red-blooded male would more than appreciate finding in his kitchen at three o'clock in the morning.

Just seeing her standing there in her nightgown stirred Reece's blood with the kind of scorching, passionate desire that he knew would haunt him long after she had returned to her bed and he to his. There had always been that chemistry between them right from the start. Reece would simply look at Sorrel and she would give him an answering look back, and before even one word was spoken they would have their hands all over each other in an instant. *It was wild…* His English Rose could be as wanton as any dark-eyed Latin lover when it came to making love.

Remembering hotly that he had taken her once right here, up against the worktop, Reece recalled that possession had been hard and fast, furious and wonderful. The scent from her heavenly body had tied his stomach up in knots and her breathless little sighs of pleasure had stoked his lust for the rest of the night. The softness of her silken thighs as he'd positioned himself between them had been sublime, and the way her innocent blue eyes had helplessly darkened and glazed to reveal the depth of her passion and need had turned Reece on so powerfully that he grew hard in an instant, just remembering the sight.

Right then the depth of the longing and lust that swirled inside him was like a hot scorching wind from the Sahara, slamming into every hidden and not so hidden corner of his body, waking him up to a desire so fierce that he trembled to contain it. Earlier, Reece had been torn between being furious that she should listen in on his phone-calls—'accidentally' or not—and feeling hope because she'd demonstrated another emotion towards him besides resentment and despair. *Sorrel had been jealous that he was meeting Angelina Cortez for lunch.* That must mean that she still felt something for him other than disdain.

'Maybe a nice massage would help?' he suggested.

The idea was heavenly—as well as terrifying. Putting down her glass of water on the drainer, Sorrel self-consciously closed her robe and tightened the narrow silky belt around her middle. This close, her gorgeous, sexy husband was a little too much on the senses to take lightly. She needed to be well armed against his almost blatant sex appeal, because she remembered where most of Reece's massages usually led. *Not that it could lead anywhere close to that heavenly destination today.* Her body was still healing. Not just her body, but her heart, her mind and her soul, too.

'Sorrel?'

She realised she hadn't answered him. She'd been so caught up in the spell of him that she'd forgotten to speak. Her blue eyes alighted apologetically on his face, helplessly drifting down to his mouth—remembering the taste and feel of his passionate lips against hers and longing to experience their touch again.

'No, it's all right. I'll just take the pills. It's nothing to make a fuss about…really.'

'You don't want me to touch you? Is that it?'

CHAPTER SIX

THERE was an undercurrent of anger as well as pure frustration contained in Reece's voice, and Sorrel wrestled with the wave of guilt that surged through her insides.

'It's…it's early days yet, Reece.'

How could she tell him that she was afraid to let him touch her?

Trying not to permit her helplessly hungry gaze to dip lower than his chest, she lifted a swathe of curling blond hair off the back of her neck and let it fall back again. There was no denying that his overpowering proximity was getting to her…

'Yeah…right.'

'I'm…I'm still healing, Reece.' Her voice went very soft, almost down to a whisper.

He gave her a lazy seductive smile that hit her straight in the solar plexus. 'I wasn't suggesting full-blown sex on the kitchen floor, angel.' He moved closer if that were possible, magnetising her attention with the shifting hue and shadow in his eyes.

If there were another man alive with such luxuriously long golden lashes they couldn't be more amazing than his.

Just one devastating glance from the sexy eyes beneath those lashes could make Sorrel's hips grow soft and the rest of her feel as though she was melting like chocolate in the heat.

Capturing one of her gently curving blond curls between his fingers, Reece stared at it for a moment, as though examining a genuine work of art. 'Truth is, Sorrel…it's driving me crazy not being able to touch you.'

'I've missed touching you, too.'

Letting go of the tendril of hair he'd captured, Reece watched it spring away from him to rest against her shoulder. Almost holding his breath, he slid his hand behind Sorrel's graceful neck, registering the infinite softness of the minute hairs at its base that added to the delicacy of her silken skin with an explosive little thrill down his spine. Moving his fingers up and down in the tiniest most gentle of strokes, he watched the colour of her eyes deepen to the colour of blue smoke instead of blue sky. Sensing her tremble, Reece became aware of the peaks of her breasts budding inside her gown.

She had always been like that with him…*instantly* responsive. He'd loved that. God, what a turn-on that had always been! *And he loved her response even more because he'd been missing such a reaction for too long a time.* How had he borne it?

'Reece?'

'What is it, baby?'

His voice wasn't exactly steady. It couldn't help but betray the voracious need that built and gathered like a summer storm inside him. Before Sorrel could reply, he eased her towards him, clasping her hips firmly in his hands and bringing them flush against his own. Her soft, surprised gasp feathered over him. His hands moved up to settle round her perfectly tiny waist—and Reece's palms were suffused with the sensual warmth of her slender body beneath her robe. Her scent—the kind you couldn't bottle—drifted over him, drowning him in a wave of erotic sensation that had the tension that had been growing steadily inside him almost snap.

Sorrel had registered the strength of her husband's arousal as soon as he had pressed her hips against his own. It had sent a spiral of need and lust ravelling inside her that made her wish that they *could*—as Reece had so graphically phrased it—have 'full-blown sex on the kitchen floor.' Her own response electrified her insides like flash lightning.

'We can't…I mean I—'

Anxiously withdrawing from the spellbinding circle of his embrace even as she spoke, Sorrel finally pulled herself completely free of him and, with her cheeks slightly flushed with heat, offered him a shaky little smile of apology.

'It's…too soon,' she explained hoarsely.

Biting back his intense frustration, Reece rubbed his hand across the flat of his naked ribcage.

'How long am I supposed to wait before you meet me halfway, Sorrel?'

Her smile disappeared, and in its place the familiar little crease between her brows that she acquired when she was perturbed about something was evident. 'It's going to take a while for me to get over what's happened to me, Reece…besides what's happening between us as a couple. You—we just need to be patient.'

Knowing that he needed to wrestle his frustration

into submission if they were going to get anywhere, Reece nevertheless couldn't help the impatience that rose up strongly inside him. 'Patient' was the one thing he was finding it hard to be around is wife. All he wanted to do was *hold* her, for God's sake! Why was she making it so damn hard for him to reach out to her and get close?

'Well, honey…my feelings are that if we wait much longer to try and rescue things between us we may well lose the chance for ever. But perhaps you're prepared to risk that? You've grown so cold, Sorrel. And it's not just losing the baby that's made you like this. I think you've forgotten how to act like a warm-blooded woman around a man. And I think it's a crying shame.'

His words made her heart sink. As well as confirming her own deep-rooted fears that she was no longer an attractive, desirable woman, they struck right at the heart of her deepest femininity. Although Sorrel despised herself for it, all she could do was retaliate with an insult.

'Don't you dare talk to me about growing cold! *You're* the one who was going to divorce me, remember? And you would have gone through with it too if you hadn't realised that I was pregnant! So don't expect me to act like I'm grateful or something because you took me back. I don't owe you a damn thing!'

His jaw going rigid, Reece silenced any further tirade she might be about to indulge in by walking away from her and slicing his hand through the air in disgust.

'To hell with it, Sorrel! And to hell with you, too!'

The room was empty of his presence just a couple of seconds later.

* * *

Declining the cup of coffee she'd been offered on arrival, Sorrel found herself a seat in the plush waiting room of the familiar model agency that she'd worked for on and off over the past few years and sat down. Picking up a magazine from the small glass table in front of her, she started to idly flick through it while she waited.

She knew she had no business telling her agent Jenny that she was available for work when she was just barely recovering from a miscarriage, but sheer desperation to get out of the house and away from the stultifying atmosphere between her and Reece had forced Sorrel to do *something* constructive. So today, when he had left to meet Angelina Cortez for lunch, instead of working on the fashion designs she'd suddenly found she had no heart for, she had contacted Jenny and got herself an appointment with a view to work.

Maybe if she returned to work full-time she might reawaken her interest in modelling again? Maybe this time she wouldn't be so quick to turn down those prestigious catwalk jobs that would take her to the fashion hotspots of the world, and would see how lucky she was to have the opportunity instead? And maybe if she approached her career with some of the same dedication that Reece had applied to his own it might serve two purposes. First of all it might help push her out of the terrible depression that had gripped her, and secondly she might just win Reece's admiration because she was at least *trying* to do something positive for herself.

If her self-esteem returned then she and Reece might have a real chance of working things out between them.

And if she could demonstrate to her husband that she was still desirable enough to be sought after as a model, then he would hopefully see that she was still the same desirable girl he had married. *She should never have pushed him away as she had in the kitchen last night, and now she deeply regretted shrilly accusing him of only wanting to stay with her because she'd found out that she was pregnant.* Especially when Reece had already made several attempts at trying to mend their relationship.

But even as her eye fell on a picture of a pretty brunette she recognised, who decorated the fashion pages of one of the best-known glossy magazines on the market, Sorrel's sudden optimism wobbled dangerously. *Could she do it?* Could she find the strength inside that she needed to rise above the devastation that had overtaken her? And could she win back her husband's love and admiration if she did so? *Dear God, she had to at least try!* All she really wanted to do was start a family with Reece and raise their children together, but for now she would sacrifice that need and go back to modelling if it meant that her marriage with Reece had a chance…

'Sorrel, darling! Come in! Sorry to have kept you waiting. Have you had a cup of coffee?'

An attractive middle-aged blonde dressed in a tailored black trouser suit put her head round the door and singled Sorrel out from the two other models who sat in the room waiting.

'I don't want any coffee, thanks.'

Minutes later, inside the beautifully decorated office—with its walls practically covered in stunning shots of models past and present and a view of a bustling King's Road outside—Sorrel pulled out the chair opposite Jenny's wide desk and sat down. Crossing her long slim legs and folding her hands a little nervously in the lap of her blue and white cotton skirt, she met the slightly unsettling hazel gaze of the woman she had known for over seven years now.

There wasn't much you could put past Jenny Taylor. If you were hiding anything the woman was sure to root it out. And Sorrel's already precarious self-confidence dipped noticeably as she realised that the older woman would probably intuit immediately that something wasn't right. *Was her brave attempt at trying to do something positive to help herself going to be squashed before it even had a chance?*

'Something's happened.' The older woman frowned, absently stirring her mug of black coffee with a tiny silver spoon but never removing her knowing gaze from Sorrel's face for even a second.

Clasping her hands even more tightly in her lap, Sorrel smiled. 'What do you mean?'

'You look a little too peaky for my liking. Lost weight, too. Is everything all right with you and that gorgeous husband of yours?'

The woman had to be psychic. The smile faded from Sorrel's coral-painted lips. 'We've had…some problems,' she admitted, praying that Jenny would pry no further than that.

'Still doesn't like you modelling…is that it?'

'We're working things out.'

'But he's still not home a lot?'

'He is at the moment.'

Uncrossing her legs, Sorrel rested one hand on the desk in front of her, her brow creasing slightly. 'I don't really want to talk about me and Reece if you don't mind, Jenny. I was rather hoping that you might have a job for me?'

'Sweetheart, I've got a couple of jobs that ordinarily you'd be just perfect for—one of them is a huge cosmetics contract, too. But I'm not going to put you forward for them when I can clearly see that you're not yourself.'

Taking a sip of her steaming beverage, Jenny considered Sorrel curiously over the lip of her mug.

Feeling herself flush a guilty scarlet, Sorrel continued to frown. 'What do you mean, you can see I'm not myself?'

'You've always been a bit of a closed book, sweetheart, and that's fine with me. Everyone deserves some privacy, God knows. But I haven't reached the grand old age of fifty-one without gaining a little bit of wisdom when it comes to reading people, and there's something going on with you that worries me. If you've got problems with your marriage then you need to make that your priority, Sorrel—not work. Too many women sacrifice relationships for careers these days. God knows, I see enough of the results of that working here! Go home, Sorrel. Have a nice long hot bath. Put something pretty on, and if your husband is home, like you say he is, then light some candles tonight, open a bottle of wine and cosy up together on the sofa. That will do you far more good than coming into work looking like death warmed up!'

Sorrel rose immediately to her feet. There wasn't much point in staying and pleading her case when she knew inside that she wasn't exactly up to returning to work just yet. *But at least she had tried.* At least she had taken a small step towards trying to get better. There was a lot of truth in what Jenny had said, too—even if Sorrel believed that Reece would probably scorn the whole 'candles and wine, cosying up on the sofa' thing with a passion because she'd been nothing but cold towards him.

Right now he was lunching with one of the most beautiful and vivacious women she had ever seen. Coming home to his wife would be like returning to a dark, cold basement after spending most of the day in dazzling sunlight. Because Jenny was also right about her looks. Her face still bore the sorrow of her recent loss, and she'd been eating so little that it was a wonder she was still standing upright. She really *had* to make more of a concerted effort to eat better. Did she really think that Reece would fancy her if she resembled a bag of bones?

Clutching her blue suede bag to her chest, Sorrel managed to find a smile. 'You *are* wise, Jenny. The truth is I haven't been very well, and I should never have wasted your time like this. I'm sorry.'

The older woman got to her feet, too. Walking round her desk, she put her arm around Sorrel and briefly squeezed the younger woman to her. 'I'm sorry to hear that, my love. And I want to assure you that turning you away right now doesn't mean I don't want you to come back and work for me, darling. I don't need anybody in place for that big contract I told you about for another six weeks yet, and you *would* be perfect for the job. Go home, get some help for whatever's wrong, then give me a ring in about a month's time and we'll talk again. OK?'

'OK.'

'And in the meantime why don't you take a holiday? Get some sun? It would probably do you the world of good!'

With Jenny's cheerful, well-meant advice ringing in her ears, Sorrel left the modelling agency offices and walked out into the surprising blaze of sunshine pouring down on a busy King's Road. Feeling her spirits rise in spite of everything, and determined to take further steps towards her own healing, rather than go back to an empty house she decided to hang around for a while and maybe do a little shopping. She wouldn't overdo it, because she was still suffering with fatigue after her ordeal and she'd been strictly advised to take things easy, but right now Sorrel wasn't interested in spending precious time browsing clothes shops. She'd much rather seek out a wonderful little bookshop she knew of, tucked away down a very exclusive little Chelsea side street. It was there in the past that she'd often discovered some of the most fascinating and unusual books on history and music that were Reece's favourite reading material....

At first he'd panicked when he'd arrived home and found the house devoid of his wife's presence. With his heart in his mouth, Reece had climbed the stairs two at a time to her bedroom and wrenched open the wardrobe doors. Finding her clothes undisturbed, the suitcases empty and her toiletries and make-up still scattered along the marble surround in the bathroom, he had allowed himself to breathe more easily.

For a few disturbing minutes there he had seriously believed the worst—that Sorrel had left him again...only this time for good. *She hadn't wanted him to go to lunch with*

Angelina. But after the angry words they'd hurled at each other in the middle of the night, Reece hadn't felt like placating her this morning either. Work was work, he'd told himself, and life couldn't come to a standstill just because they had suffered this tragedy—*or* because Sorrel was suspicious there might be something more than just professional interest between him and the opera star.

She couldn't have gone far. Maybe she'd simply needed some fresh air and had gone for a walk in the park near their home? He'd give her another hour, he decided. If there were no sign of her by then, Reece would go out and look for her.

Suddenly feeling drained of energy emotionally, he kicked off his shoes and dropped down onto the sumptuous bed that they no longer shared. Putting his arm behind his head, he lay there for several minutes just staring up at the ceiling. The sun poured in through the huge glass panels that made up one wall in a soporific beam of light and made him drowsy. Finally, weary of thinking, Reece turned onto his side, breathed in the familiar scent that Sorrel used and which lingered so evocatively on the pillow, closed his eyes and went to sleep.

Standing in the doorway of the bedroom, Sorrel put down the bookshop carrier bag that she'd brought upstairs and stared at the still, sleeping figure of her husband stretched out on the bed. She was struck by a wave of emotion so powerful that her whole body started to tremble. With his eyes closed in sleep and his hair dishevelled as a small boy's, her love for him submerged her with almost unbearable longing.

He was so strong, vital and handsome that *any* woman would be seriously elated to come home and find him there like that—caught in a moment of exquisitely poignant vulnerability, for a short time the veneer of success and ruthless ambition tamed in the surrender of sleep. *If only he'd hear her out properly and they could settle on some agreement about the way they'd live their lives in future,* Sorrel was thinking. *If only he'd come round to seeing the benefits of family life, he might relent and let them try for another baby...* But how was that possible if he really *didn't* love her any more?

Her heart jumped guiltily as Reece suddenly opened his eyes and stared at her.

'Where have you been?' he asked, his voice still edged with sleep.

'I needed to get out of the house.'

Heat seared her cheeks and probably gave her the first tinge of colour she'd had all day. Her fingers fiddled with one of the pale blue buttons on her jacket. It was extraordinary to her that she could still feel so vulnerable in front of this man, but his undoubted masculine beauty, his strength and sheer animal magnetism, could sometimes simply stop her in her tracks.

'I went for a walk and did a little shopping.'

'Oh?' Moving himself up into a sitting position, Reece drew his legs up to his chest and linked his arms round them. 'I hope you didn't overdo things. You know you've still got to take things easy for a while.'

'I know. How did your lunch go?'

She was just making conversation, Sorrel told herself. Not fishing for information about what he and Angelina had talked about. It was already a sore subject, and she really didn't want to bring it up again and make things worse.

'It went just fine.'

His surprisingly relaxed gaze swept casually up and down Sorrel's appearance with an intimate interest he didn't bother to disguise.

She'd taken extra care with her clothes today because she'd been going to meet with her agent. Instead of more casual garb, she wore a pretty blue and white long cotton skirt, a white broderie anglaise blouse, and a sky-blue fitted jacket. With her long blond hair tumbling free and lapis lazuli earrings at each earlobe, she knew she was looking better than she had in days—even if Jenny *had* professed that she looked peaky and had clearly lost weight.

'You look like summer,' Reece commented, smiling. 'Was there a reason you got all dressed up?'

Feeling helplessly guilty that she'd gone to see her agent without mentioning it to him, Sorrel carefully avoided his probing glance. 'I just wanted to cheer myself up…that's all.'

'It was a good idea. Want to come over here and talk for a while?' he invited, patting the space on the bed beside him.

Overwhelmed by his soft-voiced invitation, Sorrel panicked and reached for the bookshop carrier bag she'd left on the floor instead. 'I bought you something,' she said quickly, the heat in her cheeks deepening.

Taking the bag from her, Reece put it to one side and grabbed her hand before she could move away. 'I'll look at it later,' he promised, and tugged a little on her hand, giving Sorrel no choice but to capitulate to his suggestion and join him on the bed.

'What do you—what do you want to talk about?' she asked nervously, tucking a honey-blond curl around her ear.

Reece was thinking that he would willingly forego talking simply to just sit here a while and gaze at her. He truly believed she had the most amazing skin and eyes that he had ever seen. He hadn't been lying when he'd told her that she looked like summer—and what better way for a man to wake from sleep than to find such a vision of loveliness before him?

'Anything…everything,' he said idly, stroking his fingers around her delicate jaw.

'Are you going away again soon, Reece?' she ventured, her glance a little strained.

'What do you mean?'

'You had lunch with Angelina. You must have discussed business? Are you going to promote her next tour?'

The truth was Reece hadn't committed to any such thing. Not yet anyway. He'd told a surprised Angelina that he would think about it and let her know. When the singer had pressed him for a reason for his apparent reticence he'd finally relented and indicated to her reluctantly that he was having some personal problems at home. After that the fiery Spaniard had been all sweetness and light, her dark eyes warm and understanding as she'd advised him to take all the time he needed to sort things out—if anyone was going to promote her tour then it would be Reece and no one else.

'Nothing's settled as yet, so in answer to your question…no…I'm not going away again soon.'

Touching Sorrel's lips with the pad of his thumb, Reece slowly lifted his gaze to hers. 'Does that make you happy, Sorrel?' he asked, his voice hypnotically velvet.

CHAPTER SEVEN

'I DON'T want you to turn down work just for me.'

Sensing her withdraw behind that wall of ice she seemed so intent on keeping erected between them, Reece slid his hand behind her neck and deliberately brought her face closer to his.

'Could you stop fighting me for just one damned minute?' he asked, emerald eyes beseeching.

She stilled, and her shoulders slumped a little. Unable to halt his next action, Reece covered her surprised mouth with his own, the softness and the taste of her lips exploding onto his senses like honey from an enchanted forest, stirring all his need, passion and longing into a roaring flame that he prayed would never be extinguished.

God, how he'd missed this! She felt and tasted like no other woman… No one else could immediately elicit such exquisite mindless joy for him at a single stroke. She could make him her slave if she wanted to…that was her power. With the intoxicating scent of summer flowers flowing over him, his tongue twining with hers, sharing heat and ardour with the woman he desired beyond all others, Reece felt all his cares washed away in the sweetest sea of sensation he could dream of swimming in.

Sensing Sorrel's shuddering capitulation to the hungry possession of his lips, he experienced the first genuine moments of happiness he'd had in a long, long time. But all too soon it was over. It was Sorrel who broke the kiss…her breathing feathering over him in softly heated gasps as she pulled away, her eyes dazed and darkened, her lips with a glaze of moisture on them from their mutual exchange of passion.

'What was that for?' Her plump lower lip quivered and Reece longed to taste her mouth all over again.

'Do I need a reason to kiss my wife?'

The genuine smile he gave her in return to her question was warm and far too alluring for words. Some of the ice around Sorrel's heart had melted as if beneath the force of a blowtorch under his flawless and arousing expertise, but she was still afraid to yield to him completely. No agreements had been reached between them as yet. They hadn't even really discussed the impact of the tragedy they had suffered. How were they going to reconcile their differences unless they *really* talked about what they both wanted once and for all?

As unexpected and pleasurable as Reece's kiss had been, *one kiss does not a future make,* Sorrel realised sadly. They might share a passion that could melt the polar icecaps, but if in everything else fundamental they were complete opposites how *could* their marriage continue with any success?

Yet at the back of Sorrel's mind she heard Jenny's voice urging her to 'take a holiday, get some sun' and she couldn't help but wonder if Reece had been right when he'd made the same suggestion? Perhaps they *should* go to the house in the Algarve and get to know each other all over again? A tiny flicker of hope burst into flame inside her heart and almost begged her to take a chance.

'No…you don't need a reason.' Her reply was verging on shy, and she let him play with her fingers and circle the pad of his thumb round and round her palm. His teasing touch elicited tiny and powerful explosions of pleasure all over her body. 'Reece, I was wondering…'

'What were you wondering, sweetheart?' He smiled again, and for a moment Sorrel was struck speechless by his power to unravel her so completely with even the smallest seemingly innocent gesture.

'What you suggested a while ago…about us going away for a while to the house in the Algarve…? I've been thinking…I've been thinking that I might like that after all.'

Catching his breath in surprise at this unexpected olive branch, Reece brought Sorrel's hand up to his lips and kissed it…slowly and tenderly. When his gaze met hers again, the dazzling emerald of his eyes seemed to shine with even more clarity and brilliance.

'I'll see if I can book us on a flight out to Faro tomorrow,' he promised.

'So soon?'

'What have we got to wait for? We've only got ourselves to please.'

His words painfully and unwittingly reminded Sorrel that, yes…they *did* only have themselves to please—because there was no longer a baby to look forward to.

And the light in her eyes faded a little as she met her husband's openly pleased glance.

'OK.' She rose up from the bed before he could stop her and went to the door. 'I'll pack later. Right now I'm going to go and phone Melody before I start fixing dinner. See you downstairs.'

It was only later, when she was standing at the centre island in the big modern kitchen peeling carrots into a colander, that Sorrel wondered what Reece had been doing in her bedroom. It puzzled her. He'd removed all his clothing from the built-in wardrobes to the room he was occupying down the hall, so what reason would he have had to be in there? And why had he fallen asleep on the bed?

Recalling his kiss, she stopped mid-peel and touched her fingers to her lips. She could still feel the blazing, tingling imprint of his sexy and persuasive mouth against hers—still remember the way he'd kissed her, so slow and deep and taunting that a girl would honestly be ready to surrender not just her body but her heart and soul to him. It was one of the things Sorrel loved best about his lovemaking. He knew how to take his time, how to take her to the highest peak and give her the utmost pleasure first, before taking his own. Selfish was one thing Reece had never been as a lover…

'Sorrel?'

His voice caught her unawares, and she blushed guiltily as if he could tell at a glance just what she'd been thinking about before he appeared. He was standing in the doorway of the kitchen, shirt unbuttoned and jeans hanging low across his taut lean hips, with the merest tantalising glimpse of manly belly button, and the sight of him caused Sorrel's womb to ache almost unbearably. She leaned against the worktop to regain a sense of balance. Clearly not long out of the shower, his golden hair glistened damply, and his effortlessly sexy smile found its target immediately and set free a cage of butterflies in her stomach.

'What is it?' She started to peel the carrot in her hand at an almost frantic pace.

'We're in luck. I've booked us first-class flights out to Faro tomorrow at noon. By the time we arrive and pick up the hire car we should get to the house around six or thereabouts. How does that sound?'

'That's great.'

'I've rung Ricardo and Ines and told them to expect us, so the house should be all ready and waiting.'

The Portuguese couple that Reece employed to look after the house for them when it wasn't in use—and also to housekeep for them when it was—lived in a small traditional farmhouse about two miles from their own place. It had been quite a while since Sorrel had seen them both, and her heart lifted a little at the prospect of seeing them again. The couple had always been so kind and helpful—they could never do enough to make them comfortable, it seemed, and Reece trusted them implicitly.

'So all we have to do is pack?'

'That's right.' He came into the room and stood at the other side of the island to observe her. 'What are you doing?'

She shrugged a little self-consciously. 'I was just making us a shepherd's pie with some beans and carrots. Is that OK?'

'Honey, I don't want you tiring yourself out cooking.

You've already been out shopping today when you should have been resting. Why don't we just order a take-out?'

'I thought shepherd's pie was one of your favourites?' She couldn't prevent the small thread of hurt that wove through her voice.

'It is. I'd just really prefer you not to have to cook right now. Oh…by the way, I loved the book…thanks. It's one I was going to order myself. You must have read my mind.'

Touched at the unexpected compliment, Sorrel raised her head to smile at him. But he was already walking out through the door, whistling beneath his breath as he went…

Reece was in his room packing when the phone rang on the bedside table. Aware that Sorrel was taking a shower, he sat down beside the opened suitcase he'd left on the bed to answer it.

'Hello?'

'Reece, *mi querido*! It is Angelina here. I was so concerned about you when we met for lunch earlier today that I haven't been able to stop thinking about you. I rang up to tell you that I really think that you must take a holiday—you and your pretty wife. You have clearly been working too hard and it makes sense for you to go away and get some rest…yes?'

Genuinely touched that the renowned singer should spend time thinking about concerns not her own, Reece stared out though the glass panels at the perfect arrangement of terracotta tubs, and the chrome table and chair set out on the patio, and frowned. Ordinarily he would register the sight and not be disturbed by it. But right at that moment for some inexplicable reason the pristine arrangement of flowers and garden furniture upset him. So much so that he experienced an almost overpowering desire to go out there and mess it up a little.

'As a matter of fact we're going to do just that, Angelina.' Diverting his attention determinedly back to his caller, he sighed. 'We're flying out to Faro tomorrow and we're going to stay at a house we own nearby.'

'You are flying out tomorrow to *Faro*?'

She sounded shocked. Reece drew his dark blond brows together in a frown. 'Is there something wrong with that?'

'No, *querido,* far from it! I have a villa in Almancil, near Vale do Lobo, and Emmanuel and I are flying out there this Saturday! But this must be fate, yes? So, you must give me your number there and I will ring you and make arrangements for you and your wife to come to my house and have dinner with us. But how wonderful!'

His feelings were mixed on whether it would be wise to give Angelina his Portuguese phone number, and Reece rubbed at the crease between his brows and sucked in a lightly troubled breath.

He wondered what Sorrel would think about an invitation to dinner at the sultry diva's luxury residence? Would she think that he'd planned the whole going to the Algarve thing just so that he might 'bump into' Angelina? But then he remembered that it had been Sorrel, not he, who had instigated their trip, and he breathed out again with relief. If Sorrel got to meet the star properly, he reflected, she might come to see that actually Angelina wasn't the slightest bit interested in Reece as a potential conquest but genuinely thought of him as a friend. In light of that, what harm would it do to give her the telephone number?

They arrived at the house Reece had christened Paradise na Terra—Paradise on Earth—at around six-thirty in the evening. As expected, Ricardo and Ines had worked hard in preparation for their visit.

The old converted farmhouse, with its huge immaculately mown lawned gardens, roof terrace and traditional architecture, very much reflected old style grace and beauty on this slightly cooler spring evening when Reece and Sorrel drove into the courtyard. A dazzling array of exotic plants and flowers perfumed the air and the house fair shone with love and devotion even before they took a step inside. It had been a bumpy flight out from Heathrow, and—her nerves already strung tight at the thought of spending uninterrupted time with her husband, given the tense situation between them—Sorrel was very glad to just arrive and be able to sit down.

Leaving their suitcases in the open covered porch outside the first reception room, Reece led Sorrel to the nearest couch and told her to put her feet up. Concerned that she looked particularly pale and tired after their long journey, he knew she really needed to listen to his advice and just rest until it was time to eat.

Heading into the large, colourful kitchen, in which Ines's invaluable local knowledge of all things domestic had contributed to the design, Reece was gratified to find a meal ready and waiting on the kitchen table and a bottle of local wine with a corkscrew and two large wine glasses standing beside it. Helping himself to some black olives, he shrugged off his jacket and stared out of the window, his attention captured by the beauty of the serene landscape and the blazing orange sun preparing to set, hovering above the hills on the horizon.

A peace of sorts descended on him. He couldn't quite put his finger on it, but he couldn't discount the feeling either. Maybe he and Sorrel were right where they needed to be? Reece thought. Maybe here, somehow, some way, they could finally begin to mend what was broken between them? This enforced break of theirs was perhaps what had been needed all along?

If only Reece hadn't been so determinedly stubborn that his work should come first. Away from the bustle of city life, the constant travelling and wall-to-wall meetings that denoted his daily experience in general, he might remember what it was like to be content with the simpler things in life. Like taking a walk in the woods or watching the sunset. He might learn how to enjoy just 'being' instead of 'doing' for a while, and not constantly try to seek happiness in the sometimes hollow rewards of his ambition. He might also get to reacquaint himself with the company of the beautiful, quixotic woman he had fallen in love with.

'I'm hungry,' Sorrel announced behind him as she padded barefoot onto the large square tiles of the terracotta floor.

She too had removed her linen jacket; underneath she wore a simple long white broderie anglaise shift dress. With her honey-blond hair swept up behind her head, and exquisite tendrils floating loose around a face more or less bare of make-up, she appeared very young and very sweet.

A strong jolt of awareness and protection knifed unexpectedly through Reece's chest as he studied her. For a moment he experienced a flash of how she'd looked the night she had lost the baby—in a white nightgown not dissimilar to the dress she was wearing now, but stained horribly and sickeningly with blood... His insides reacted with abhorrence at the jarring memory and for a moment he was so stricken he couldn't speak.

'Reece?'

Aware that he was miles away, Sorrel felt her heart skip a beat. *Was he regretting coming away with her when things between them had been so bad? Was he concluding that this whole excursion was probably futile?* Not wanting to travel down such horribly familiar highways of heartbreak on their first night away together, she dragged her gaze determinedly away from the preoccupied expression crossing his handsome face and instead registered the sumptuous spread of food laid out on the table before her.

'Did Ines do all this?'

Snapping out of the trance he'd been in, Reece popped a fat glistening olive into his mouth and groaned appreciatively as the sublime taste and texture drowned his tastebuds in unadulterated pleasure.

'Sure did. The woman's one of God's own angels!'

Sorrel loved it when he displayed his pleasure. He didn't hold back like some men did. Whether it was food, wine, a beautiful painting, or sex...Reece knew how to show his appreciation. Her head felt giddy at the thought.

'Why don't we take the food outside?' she suggested, leaning over the square pine table to gather up a platter of fruit, cheese and olives.

'Isn't it a little cool?' Reece asked, catching her eye. He couldn't help wondering why she suddenly appeared to be blushing, and he was immediately intrigued.

'I can put my jacket on—or I've got a wrap in my shoulderbag.'

'Fine. Let's do it.'

They sat in an unexpectedly companionable silence for almost an hour, watching the sun finally disappear and the strategically placed fairylights that Ricardo had arranged around the porch for their benefit automatically come on. Reece had wanted all-singing, all-dancing, high-tech everything when it came to the lighting in that area, but Sorrel had loved Ricardo's simple suggestion of fairy-lights, declaring them to lend a much more magical air of enchantment than anything more modern.

Now, as she sat sipping her wine, watching the changing light create new shadows and intriguing angles on her husband's compelling features, she noticed that some of the light grooves on his brow and round his mouth had definitely deepened. As though a troubled artist had taken his palette knife and gouged out more definite lines. A hollow, tight feeling cramped her stomach, and Sorrel couldn't help but feel mournful at the knowledge that Reece had suffered equally at the sad decline of their relationship as well as at the dreadful ensuing loss of the baby she'd been carrying. He'd told her as much but she hadn't really been listening at the time. She'd been too wrapped up in her own bruising pain.

If their marriage hadn't been at the point of no return when Sorrel had suffered the miscarriage, maybe they could have comforted each other more, she reflected, sipping a little more wine to numb her hurt. Now they were both in the land of lost relationships—both desperately trying to find a way out of their shared misery and neither one of them willing to make the first move towards shattering the remembered bond of love that they had so delighted in at the beginning.

'You didn't eat very much.' His voice broke into her melancholy reverie as Reece glanced at the still nearly full platters of food on the table, then back at Sorrel.

'Neither did you.'

'I think I'd rather just drink some more wine right now,' he confessed, his mouth nowhere near a smile.

Sorrel swallowed hard. Was he drinking to numb his pain?

'Now that we're here,' she questioned him bluntly, 'do you regret coming?'

Reece's answering glance was equally if not more blunt. 'Not at all. But, like you said before, Sorrel, it takes two to commit fully to a relationship. I don't intend on walking on eggshells around you while we try and work things out.'

'I'm not asking you to "walk on eggshells" around me! And I can take criticism if I'm wrong, too. I'm tougher than I look, you know.'

Unable to prevent the speculative grin that broke loose from his lips, Reece lifted his feet onto another wrought-iron chair and glanced at her indignant expression with amusement. '*Tough* is not a word I'd use to describe you, angel…at least not the way I see it. Right now you look like a child who's stayed up way past her bedtime. Want me to come and tuck you into bed?'

His mention of the one word which was loaded with all kinds of meaning that Sorrel would much prefer to shy away from—*bed*—had her spine going immediately rigid and her hand once more reaching for her wine glass. 'No, thank you! In any case I'm *not* a child—and I'm perfectly capable of deciding what time I go to bed.'

'Prickly as a porcupine as usual,' Reece taunted, smiling, but Sorrel glared right back at him.

'No, I'm not!'

'See?'

The sound of his husky-voiced laugh rippled over her nerve endings like rich maple syrup being poured over ice-cream and made her shiver. Seeing her rub her bare arms up and down, Reece was immediately contrite. 'You're cold. Let's go inside.'

Feeling slightly guilty that he should interpret her trembling as the effects of cold, Sorrel turned round to collect her jacket from her chair, but rather than put it on draped it around her shoulders. 'I'm fine now. I'd rather stay out here for a while than go inside.'

Her shivering didn't stop. With Reece's unsettling heated gaze drifting intently over her features, then slowly, unashamedly moving down to the slight shadow between her breasts in the simple sleeveless white dress, Sorrel knew who had the upper hand in this little *tête-à tête* they were having. And it *wasn't* her.

'You *are* cold, Sorrel…I can see the evidence for myself.'

Glancing down at her chest and seeing the clear outline of her peaked nipples pressing against the thin material of her lace bra and the even thinner material of her dress, she chewed down on her lip in genuine embarrassment.

'Must you bring everything down to the lowest common denominator?' she demanded.

'You're a beautiful, sexy woman, Sorrel...why do you think I was attracted to you in the first place? Am I supposed not to notice the intimate little things about you any more? Like the way your blue eyes turn dark and smoky when you're aroused...the way your body moves—so graceful you almost glide...or the way your scent leaves a sexy trail behind you when you exit a room? Do you think that I'm dead from the waist down now that you've made me public enemy number one?'

CHAPTER EIGHT

'I DON'T think of you as my enemy!' she retaliated, stung. But her indignation was due in part to the fact that his beguiling words had left her stranded all at sea, without a tow rope to guide her safely back to harbour.

To cover her confusion, she pushed to her feet and started to lift one of the abundant platters. 'You're right—it *is* getting chilly out here. I think I'll clear these dishes away, then go and unpack my things.'

Biting back his undeniable and increasingly impatient need to have her demonstrate a little warmth towards him, Reece tried not to let his intense frustration with the situation spill over into another argument. Lifting his glass, he tipped it slightly from side to side to let the alcohol roll around inside rather than put it straight to his lips.

He knew that yet again Sorrel was running away from her discomfort with him. And if his anger made her uncomfortable, then his compliments seem to make her discomfort even *worse. What the hell was a guy supposed to do?* All Reece knew was that he would pay a lot of money to reverse the situation, because right now it honestly had him stumped.

'Leave the dishes. I'm just going to sit out here for a while and come in when I'm ready.'

Exchanging one last heated glance with her slightly guilty blue gaze, Reece finally raised his glass to his lips and drank deeply of the robust little Portuguese red that Ines had so thoughtfully left them to enjoy with their meal.

Wrapped in her white towelling robe, Sorrel stepped out of the bathroom into the bedroom to find Reece hanging some linen shirts in the vast antique wardrobe. As he reached forward to position the wooden hangers the muscles in his back rippled underneath the plain black T-shirt he wore, and suddenly all the moisture in Sorrel's mouth seemed to dry up like an unused well.

'What are you doing?' she asked, her heart beginning to pound.

He turned only briefly. 'What do you *think* I'm doing? I'm hanging up my clothes in the closet.'

'You're going to sleep in here—with me?' Her gaze went nervously to the big double bed with its traditional embroidered quilt.

'That's right. You got any problems with that?'

They hadn't shared a bed in over three months…nearly four. Was he really treating his return to their bedroom so casually? As if it had hardly any significance at all?

'There are two other bedrooms in the house, and I'm sure Ines will have made up all the beds.'

That got his attention. Turning slowly, his hands on his hips, Reece looked at her hard. 'So?'

'I just don't think it's a very good idea to try and force the issue…do you?'

'I'm not trying to *force* anything, dammit!'

After turning away briefly, to try and calm the fury that swirled in his chest, Reece swung his glance back to Sorrel and swept it up and down her robed figure almost with disdain. 'I may not be your idea of the perfect gentleman, honey, but even *I* wouldn't try and force my wife into an intimacy she doesn't welcome. Please give me some credit! But this situation will soon be going way past the point where anything can be rescued if we don't do something to rectify it. All I want to do is share a bed together again. At least let's agree on that, shall we?'

Trying desperately hard to be objective in the midst of a sea of emotion that threatened to swamp her, Sorrel studied Reece's straight up and down muscular physique and arrestingly handsome features with the slow, insistent throb of sensual awareness creeping stealthily into her blood.

She knew that any other woman would probably be thrilled with the idea that such a man was apparently so determined to share her bed, and in her secret heart Sorrel was not immune to similar excitement either. But how *could* she be objective when she was so affected by practically *everything* this man did? When he sighed anxiety gripped her over what might be wrong. When he laughed in happiness and without restraint she knew joy unbounded. On the outside it shouldn't be so complicated to invite him back into her bed again. But on the *inside*...Sorrel saw nothing but difficulty ahead.

She wasn't ready. She had nothing to give him, nothing to offer. How could she when inside her there was nothing but a big empty void since she had lost their baby?

'Sorrel?'

'You'll have to please yourself. I—I can't think straight right now. I'm tired and all I want to do is go to sleep.'

Watching in disbelief and bitter disappointment as she turned around and walked back into the bathroom, Reece stared down at the mosaic-tiled floor beneath his bare feet and for a long moment could see nothing but a red mist swirling in front of his eyes. Then—resigning himself to another cold, torturous lonely night—he yanked his shirts back out of the wardrobe, picked up his suitcase and slammed out of the room to go to another bedroom further down the hall.

At the sound of the door being practically slammed off its hinges, Sorrel stared at her pale, anxious reflection in the bathroom mirror and couldn't help but *despise* what she saw there….

In contrast to the cool of the previous evening, the following day the sun beat down on the cobbled pavements of the small Portuguese coastal town with—to Sorrel's mind, at least—the same burning intensity with which it blazed down on the pyramids of Egypt.

Wearing a straw hat with a yellow silk daffodil pinned to the side, white drawstring trousers and a cinnamon-coloured cotton camisole, she was forced to reduce her walk to a slow, leisurely amble whether she wanted to or not. In comparison, the heat hardly seemed to affect Reece at all. In dark sunglasses, khaki trousers and white linen shirt, his golden hair gleaming like an eye-catching halo, he strode around like a beautiful sun god who had touched down briefly on earthly soil to visit. It aggrieved Sorrel to notice the covetous glances he received from the local girls and female tourists alike, and she tried to focus on the scenery instead.

Up ahead, at the end of the long narrow cobbled road they were walking, they came face to face with the most stunning church. Ornate and shining in the midday sun, its high roofs and bold edifice were set in such a position as to do nothing less than simply command the utmost and awed attention of any onlooker.

'Can we go inside?' Sorrel asked Reece as he stopped and shielded a hand over the top of his sunglasses to take a look.

'Sure. Why not?'

He was speaking to her…but only *just*. Last night he'd made another concerted effort to try and bring them closer together—and what had Sorrel done? *She'd rebuffed him again.* In light of that, she could hardly expect him to be overly pleasant or communicative. So now, even though she knew it was her fault, Sorrel couldn't find a lot of joy in either the beautiful day *or* the charming scenery. It was as though her mind and her heart were locked away inside a dark, narrow box and she couldn't find the key to open it and let in the daylight.

Watching him stride ahead, she saw a young slim Portuguese girl stand to one side of the wide narrow steps that led inside the church turn her head and make no secret of her admiration as Reece walked casually by. She didn't even acknowledge *her*. A little spurt of jealousy and pride throbbed inside Sorrel's chest as she moved to catch up with him, the sudden exertion drenching her back with heat.

Inside the imposing edifice it was blissfully cool, with the strong, pungent scent of incense hanging hypnotically in the air. Standing at the beginning of the long narrow aisle that cut a swathe through the middle of the church, both Sorrel and Reece turned their heads this way and that to examine the awe-inspiring religious art that decorated the ancient walls. Then, moving towards a small side chapel, where candles were burning on a wrought-iron stand in front of a beautifully ornate statue of the Virgin Mary, Sorrel searched in her purse for some change and positioned one of the candles carefully in an empty holder to light.

Watching his wife through the gothic-style archway that led into the chapel as she lit the little candle, Reece was momentarily mesmerised by the sight of her. She had removed her straw hat on entering the church, and her bright blond hair was backlit by a ray of sunlight streaming in through a stained glass window—she looked almost heartstoppingly beautiful and very young. *Too young*, Reece thought as emotion welled up inside him. Too young to have lost a longed-for baby and to have suffered a night of terror as she had when she'd lost it.

Because he now knew with unequivocal doubt that Sorrel had wanted that baby more than anything else…*maybe even more than she wanted their marriage to continue.* He absorbed the stinging realisation with a deeply heavy sigh of profound regret. Another woman with the same wonderful opportunities to travel and have such a glamorous career as fashion modelling might have resented the looming curtailment of that career in lieu of taking care of a child…but not Sorrel. Motherhood would come naturally to her, and she wouldn't resent the responsibility one iota.

'She looks like the Madonna, no?' A smiling Italian tourist, his sunglasses on the top of his head and his bronzed tan evident even in the dim interior of the church, stopped next to Reece to gaze in mutual admiration at Sorrel as she stood in front of the several rows of flickering candles, her expression rapt.

Reece couldn't even find the words to answer him. But he did find a quickening of longing take an almost violent hold inside him as he shared the vision of his beautiful wife with the unknown tourist and desired nothing more than to take her home and keep her for nobody else's edification other than his own. Giving the other man a brief nod of acknowledgement, he moved into the little chapel to step up beside Sorrel. He already knew the answer to the question he was about to ask her, but somehow he was driven to hear confirmation of it from her own lips.

'Who did you light the candle for?'

His voice was pitched low so that only she could hear. Turning to glance at him, Sorrel clutched her straw hat with the jaunty little silk daffodil to her chest and gave him the briefest glimpse of a tiny smile.

'Our baby,' she whispered, and Reece saw her lovely blue eyes glaze over with unshed tears. Fighting back the wave of inconsolable sorrow that flooded his heart, he put his hand behind her waist, and as he did so the intoxicating scent of rose stirred the air—for a moment shutting out the more sonorous smell of incense that was everywhere.

It hit Reece right in the centre of his solar plexus and

brought an immediate almost shockingly accurate vision of his mother to mind. He stopped still and didn't move. *His mother had always smelled of roses. They had been her favourite flowers.*

'Reece?'

Having turned and caught the shocked glance of surprise mirrored in her husband's stunning green eyes, Sorrel felt her heartbeat quicken with concern. 'Is everything all right?'

'What perfume are you wearing?' he asked huskily.

More than a little discomfited, Sorrel shrugged. 'I'm not wearing any perfume today…why?'

Seemingly snapping out of the trance he appeared to have fallen into, Reece flashed her a genuinely warm smile. 'It doesn't matter, honey. Let's go, shall we?'

Somehow feeling that he'd been given a rare gift, but not really understanding how or why, Reece led his wife gently away from the undoubted peace of the exquisite little chapel to the shimmering haze of the hot afternoon outside.

Ricardo and his plump, unashamedly expressive wife Ines were waiting for Reece and Sorrel on their return. When they drew up outside the house in their hire car Ines flew out of the kitchen, where she'd been working, and Ricardo appeared from one of the terraces to greet them. As tall and thin as his wife was short and round, with his face a deep bronze ingrained by the sun and his crinkling brown eyes, he looked as if he was a quintessential part of the earthy landscape surrounding them. He was also the kind of man who would willingly lend a hand or put his shoulder to the wheel for anybody in need and expect nothing in return.

With great enthusiasm and warmth he pumped Reece's

hand, then embraced him, and did the same to Sorrel. But it was Ines's great motherly hug that almost made Sorrel dissolve into tears. The woman had five grown-up children of her own and several grandchildren, and her stores of energy, enthusiasm and affection were seemingly boundless.

'Minha crianca doce! My sweet child!' she crooned, touching Sorrel's face and stroking her hair—as if indeed she really *were* a child. 'But you have got so thin! What is this? You do not eat any more? Tell me?'

Catching Reece's eye across his wife's shoulder, Ines looked to him to give her an explanation for what she clearly concluded was Sorrel's unacceptable slenderness.

'I can't get her to eat, Ines,' he confessed, with no small regret in his tone. 'Perhaps you can do better and tempt her with your wonderful cooking while we are here?'

'Yes, yes! She must eat! This is not good she is so thin! I have made one of my best dishes for you both tonight, and if you do not enjoy it you will break my heart!' she announced dramatically.

Ricardo nodded sagely. 'She is right. Food is a great healer when you are having troubled times,' he added, exchanging a secret glance of mutual understanding.

His hands on his hips, Reece frowned for a moment. It seemed it was a day for strange happenings. First the strong sense of his mother's presence back in the little church, and now this. How Ricardo and Ines had intuited that he and Sorrel had been having 'troubled times' he didn't rightly know, since he had not mentioned any such thing to the couple at all.

'I promise I will enjoy your lovely cooking tonight, Ines. I will make a great effort especially for you. But right now I think I need to get out of the sun for a little while. Do you mind?' Sorrel squeezed Ines's plump bronzed hand with genuine apology. 'I'm feeling a little tired, and I might just go and have a lie-down.'

'Is there anything I can get for you, my child? Perhaps a long cool drink? I will bring it to your room.' Ines immediately bustled away in search of the kitchen.

As she turned away herself, towards the house, Sorrel felt Reece's hand on her arm.

'Are you OK?' he demanded, clearly concerned that she needed to lie down.

'Yes, I'm fine,' she assured him, not quite meeting his gaze. 'I've just got a slight headache, that's all. I'm not used to the sun yet.'

'Then go and rest. I'll come in and check on you later,' he said, and let his arm drop to his side.

She hadn't been lying when she'd told him that the sun had made her feel tired. But emotion was also weighing her down, making her feel weary and permanently close to tears. In the little chapel today, when she had lit the candle and offered up a prayer for her baby, Sorrel had wondered how she was supposed to go on living when a permanent cloud of sadness seemed to be dogging her every step. She and Reece were still no closer to resolving their difficulties—and how long would he wait, she wondered, before he thought enough was enough and concluded that perhaps a divorce *was* the only real solution to their problems? He was a dynamic, vital man, with a man's healthy needs, and no doubt there'd be no shortage of interested women to help him meet them should he decide to end their marriage.

Closing her eyes against the pain of her own tormenting thoughts, she turned her face into the pillow and prayed for sleep to give her a brief respite from her seemingly endless sorrow.

It was a terrible dream—even more graphic in content than when she had experienced the real thing. Clutching the bedcover to her as sweat trickled down between her breasts and clung to her forehead, Sorrel finally threw the sheet aside, sat up and swung her legs over the edge of the bed. Staring down at her long pink nightgown, which was made out of the same material as a T-shirt, she at last woke up to the fact that everything was as it should be. There was no distressing sight of blood, as there had been in her dream, and she wasn't in any kind of physical pain. No. It was the *emotional* and *spiritual* pain that was threatening to take her breath away.

Crossing her arms in front of her stomach, Sorrel leant forward and rocked to and fro in a keening rhythm as old as time, trying desperately to contain the grief and distress that poured out of her heart. She was like a wounded animal run to ground, with not a single solitary person to care that she was so distressed or hurt. Her very soul cried out for strong arms to hold her, to witness her pain without words and merely be an ally in the searing silence until such time as she could breathe again and return to herself. *Reece.*

Without even realising that she had got to her feet, Sorrel headed for the door and went out into the quiet corridor with its cool tiled floor. In her bare feet she found herself walking towards the room a little way down from hers, opening the door and staring at Reece's prone figure beneath the single Egyptian cotton sheet on the bed, outlined only by the light of the moon that shone through the uncovered window and the dim light that illuminated him from the corridor behind her. One bare golden arm was flung out by his side, and the sheer strength and beauty of the man made her shiver violently.

Suddenly unsure whether she should have come to him after all, Sorrel nearly jumped out of her skin when Reece opened his eyes, propped himself up on one elbow and studied her with immediate concern reflected across his compelling face. 'What's wrong?'

Hesitating for only a moment, Sorrel shut the door behind her and moved across the room to stand beside the bed.

'Will you hold me?' she asked him. Her throat almost closed with pain on the words.

Needing no more entreaty than that, Reece reached out for her hand and pulled her down next to him. 'Get in,' he said hoarsely.

Climbing beneath the sheet, heavy with the warmth from his vital strong body, Sorrel lay down with her back to him and let him pull her tight against his chest. As his heat and strength enfolded her, the familiar male scent from his body saturating her senses and the fine silken hairs on his muscled arms feeling like heaven beneath her fingers, Sorrel started to shudder with the force of emotion that swept through her.

'Let it out, baby,' Reece crooned next to her ear. 'Let it all out. I'm here now…I'm here.'

CHAPTER NINE

EVERY quiver, every shudder, was like a knife carving his heart into tiny little pieces. Holding her hard against him, he held onto her slender trembling body like a lifeguard held onto someone who was nearly drowning. Reece wanted to weep, too—not just for the tragedy that had befallen their expected baby, but also for the loss of the trust and the love they had once shared so passionately.

Feeling the whisper-soft hair that spread out on the pillow beside him touch his skin, Reece breathed Sorrel in, closing his eyes to the pain and the pleasure of her closeness…a closeness he had missed more than anything he had ever lost in his life before. *Only the loss of his mother matched it.*

'Try and sleep now, honey. I'm here for you, and I promise you I'm not going anywhere.'

Touching his lips to her hair, he made a silent vow that, come earthquake, thunder or flood, he would hold her tight to him for the rest of the night if she allowed it. As Sorrel continued to sob into the pillow Reece knew that no other words were necessary….

* * *

Bright sunlight streaming in through the uncovered window made Sorrel open her eyes extra slowly. There was some kind of weight pinning her down, and when she realised that it was Reece's arm anchored across her chest she couldn't help but release a gasp. She had slept as if she'd been heavily sedated, hardly stirring a muscle. Now it shocked her to remember that she had come into his bedroom of her own volition—in search of comfort and solace because of the soul-searing nightmare that had punctured her sleep. *And he'd held her and kept her safe all night.*

Unsure of what she would say to him when he woke, she stared up the ceiling, trying to buy some time and wishing that her head didn't throb so much. But, as well as the ache in her temples, there was another part of her anatomy that was waking up to an ache, too—but this one wasn't painful. The physical need that seemed to be gripping her because of the intimate proximity of her husband's strong, fit, warm body took Sorrel by complete surprise. It had been such a long time since they had shared a bed that she'd forgotten how arousing it could be—especially first thing in the morning.

Slightly moving her leg, she felt the naked muscle of Reece's strong thigh brush against her, and heat just seemed to pour into her from everywhere. He groaned softly beside her as he started to surface from sleep, and as he moved his arm his hand glanced against Sorrel's breast beneath her nightwear. An electrical shock couldn't have stunned her senses more. Biting her lip, she hardly dared draw breath, even as her nipple hardened into a small tight pebble. Then he was raising his head and smiling at her, his expression downright lascivious.

The effect was the equivalent of an explosive sexual broadside on a libido slumbering peacefully in relatively calm waters. Blinking back the searing effects of the riveting emerald gaze that was practically blinding her with its intensity, Sorrel's intended smile of greeting barely made it to her lips. 'Good morning,' she said huskily.

It *had* to be a good morning if Sorrel was back in his bed, Reece thought with no small amount of fierce pleasure. *And she was there of her own free will.* Remembering the events of the night with an undeniable throb of warmth in his chest, he stroked back a deliciously wanton honey-blond curl from his wife's pale, smooth brow and felt a rush of helpless heat flood his loins when he saw her pretty blue eyes turn that smoky shade that told him she was aroused.

'Good morning to you too, beautiful.'

'We should get up. I'm in desperate need of a cup of tea.'

'And I'm desperately in need of…a kiss.'

Before she could respond to such an unexpected declaration, Reece lowered his head and planted a slow, burning kiss on Sorrel's surprised mouth. As his velvet tongue stroked her into compliance, her heart went delirious with delight, her hips turned soft and needy, and the ache in her breasts almost made her want to crawl out of her skin. *The man must have taken lessons from no less than a master seducer,* she concluded dazedly, her lips throbbing and clamouring for more of the same wicked treatment. Even in the morning Reece tasted good. He smelled good, too—

all warm and musky and deliciously, gorgeously masculine.

'Hmm…that was nice.'

He was circling one of her breasts with his fingers, watching the nipple pucker and grow tight beneath the pink material of her nightwear with absorbed fascination. Letting out a shaky breath, Sorrel frowned. As explosively arousing as his touch undoubtedly was, she wasn't ready for this sexual bombardment of the senses he was drugging her with. *And what could she do about it anyway?* She still had nearly three weeks to go before she could safely make love. They'd both only end up feeling frustrated, and how would that help either of them?

Feeling doubt and sudden fear shiver through her, Sorrel deliberately dragged her glance away from the hot, simmering promise in his eyes. 'I've got to get up.'

'What's your hurry, angel? We're on vacation…remember?'

'I—I need the bathroom.'

'Sure you're not just running away?'

In the middle of circling her aroused nipple, Reece stopped his sensual teasing and successfully trapped her gaze. Unsettled by the suspicion she saw lurking there, Sorrel pushed herself up into a sitting position and threaded her fingers nervously through her dishevelled blond hair.

'Running away?'

'From us…from intimacy. We don't need to actually go all the way to enjoy being intimate, Sorrel. There are lots of things I can do for you to make you feel good.'

His honeyed words started an ache down deep inside

her that begged her to allow him to demonstrate. *Oh, how she thrilled to hear him suggest that he still wanted to please her sexually!* But underlying Sorrel's pleasure, threatening to drag her straight back down into the murky darkness, was a deep feeling of inadequacy and fear. Not being able to bear the child of the man she loved struck at the most profound core of a woman's femininity. How could she possibly deserve pleasure when she felt so bad about herself? She clearly wasn't good enough in some way, or else why would this terrible thing have happened to her?

Was she being punished because she'd wanted too much of her husband's time and attention? Reece had always told Sorrel that he worked hard for her, too, because he didn't want her to be denied anything her heart desired. *But what if her desire was to have a baby and a husband who was home more often than he was away? A husband who wanted to be an integral part of the little family they'd created?*

'I…I enjoyed you holding me last night, Reece, I really did. But I'm not ready for anything more intimate than that. To tell you the truth…I'm so *scared* of us being intimate again. I've got all these terrifying feelings inside me about losing the baby and not feeling good enough, and I don't know what to do with them. My own body betrayed me, and sometimes I think the fear is making me crazy! Please don't think I was using you in any way…I—I just needed you to hold me for a while.'

'Why didn't you tell me what was wrong? I could have helped you, Sorrel. I still can. We can even see someone while we're in Portugal. I have lots of contacts…people I can ask for advice to find the best person to help. You're not in this alone, honey…I've been trying to tell you that all along. Don't shut me out. Now that I know what you're feeling I won't pressure you.'

He'd registered the pain behind her words with staggering regret. Yet he couldn't deny his own frustration at not being able to be intimate with his beautiful wife. There was fear underlying *his* frustration too. If they left it much longer to reach out to each other what hope would there be for their future together? Reece wanted to demonstrate to her how much he cared, how much he shared her sorrow, but at the end of the day he was only a man—and God knows his patience was testing him to the max when it came to not being able to touch Sorrel in the way he longed to touch her…

A little of the tension that had gathered between her shoulderblades left her, and Sorrel allowed herself a soft sigh. She could tell that Reece was disappointed with not being able to get as close as he apparently desired, but she saw understanding and compassion in his eyes, too, and that gave her tremendous hope. And the truth of the matter was that some part of her knew he had suffered their loss as deeply and as tragically as she had. His commitment to his work might have blinded him to some of Sorrel's more heartfelt needs, but Reece wasn't by nature a cold individual. If he said he was hurting then it must be true. Only Sorrel didn't know how to reach out to her husband and comfort him…not when she couldn't even comfort herself.

'Thank you. I'm glad that you understand how I feel. I *do* need some help, Reece…but let me seek it out when I feel ready. Is that all right?'

'We'll take it one step at a time. Nobody's pushing you to do anything you're not ready for. We've been to hell and back, Sorrel, and I know things aren't just going to slot back into place as easily as we might wish them to. But if we work together we can make some important headway, don't you think?'

Oh, God! If he only knew how much she would like that! Struggling to find her feet again and win back her self-esteem on her own clearly *wasn't* the answer. And if Reece was more than willing to make the difficult journey back to wholeness with her, then Sorrel knew she could get well again.

She smiled shyly at him. 'Yes…yes, I do. Shall I go and make us some tea now?'

For answer, Reece tugged on her arm and pulled her back down beside him. 'Let me hold you for a little while longer first, huh?'

He was lying on a sun-lounger by the glistening pale blue water of the swimming pool when he heard the phone ring. Reluctant to move from the drowsy reverie he had fallen into, Reece walked across the terrace and through the opened patio doors of the living room in his bare feet.

Angelina Cortez was the owner of the hypnotically diverting tones that greeted him, and automatically Reece swept his gaze towards the other side of the terrace, where Sorrel was in conversation with Ricardo as he watered the surrounding plants. He told himself he shouldn't feel the least bit guilty that a valuable client was ringing him at his private house when he was on vacation, but he knew that Sorrel wouldn't see it like that.

Ever since she'd come into his room the other night, and Reece had held her tight as she'd wept, the glances she had given him had been as wary and trepidatious as a young doe that suspected it was being stalked by a predator—as if she hardly dared believe that they could make the important headway that Reece had talked about.

Yet there had been an unexpected breakthrough when Sorrel had admitted that she was scared and didn't feel good enough. For a few moments there she had let him into her private world of pain and admitted that she needed help. The fears she had articulated to him had cut Reece to the quick. She was such a stunning, lovely young woman, with so much to offer, and yet right now she felt none of those life-affirming things. Losing the baby had opened a wound deep inside her, and he wondered if it would ever be healed. What was worse, he barely knew what was the right thing to do to help her—and if ultimately it would be the help she truly needed at all…

'Did you have a good flight out?' Reece forced himself to ask the Spanish singer now, as she told him that she and her small son were both now in Portugal.

'Perfect! It is so good to be here and in my lovely villa again! I am ringing to remind you of my invitation to dinner, *mi querido*. Can you and your wife come tomorrow night at seven? Do you have a pen? I will give you the address.'

When Reece came back out onto the terrace by the pool, Sorrel had settled herself in the sun-lounger beside his and opened her book. She glanced up at him from behind her sunglasses as he sat down. 'Who was on the phone?'

Unable to prevent the tension that snaked across his midsection, Reece tried to keep his tone as neutral as possible. *He'd told her a while ago that he wasn't prepared to walk on eggshells around her, but wasn't that what he was doing now?* The thought couldn't help but infuriate him.

'A client.' He picked up the newspaper that lay on the little wrought-iron table between them and glanced unseeingly at the front page.

'You told them you were on holiday?' She looked perplexed—that familiar little worry line appearing between her brows.

'This is a very important client, Sorrel. There are some people I can't simply ignore.'

His words were laced with underlying annoyance, and Sorrel wondered if he was resenting this enforced vacation with a wife who every time he tried to get close just seemed to push him away. Not only that, but she was actively preventing him from getting on with his work…the job he loved.

Unhappiness descended with a vengeance. 'You know what we've been through—yet you would still put your client's needs first?'

Reece could hardly believe what he was hearing, when just the other morning in bed she had agreed that they would work together to try and sort out their problems.

'Dammit, woman! What the hell do you want from me?'

Throwing the unwanted newspaper aside, Reece pushed to his feet and stared down at Sorrel with a furious gaze. At the other side of the terrace—out of the corner of his eye—he saw a surprised Ricardo make a discreet exit.

'I'm doing my best here! Isn't it enough for you that I've taken the time out to be with you as well as expressing my desire to try and put things right? Must every damn thing I do or say to you be some kind of test I have to pass before you deign to show me a little affection or respect? If this is the way you intend to carry on, Sorrel, then maybe you were right—maybe we *should* have gone through with the damn divorce!'

'I'm sorry if that's the way you see it.'

'No, you're not! You're not sorry at all! All you want to do is wallow in your own unhappy misery and drag me down, too! Well, to hell with it! If you don't pull yourself together soon, then we may as well call it a day.'

Not waiting to hear her response—or indeed even *caring* right then what it might be—Reece strode away and disappeared inside the patio doors before Sorrel could call him back.

Her hand shook as she tried to apply the pretty rose-coloured lipstick in front of the bathroom mirror. All last night and most of the present day Reece had practically ignored her—except to tell her in almost dictatorial terms that they were going to be Angelina Cortez's dinner guests that evening, at her villa in Almancil, near Vale do Lobo.

To say she'd been shocked to learn that Angelina was in Portugal at the same time as they were was pretty inadequate to describe the state of her feelings. Sorrel's heart had slammed so hard against her ribs at the news that she'd wondered the whole of the country couldn't detect her distress. *Had they planned this little invitation between them?* They must have. Reece had to have told the opera star that he was going to be in the country with his wife, or how else would she have got his telephone number there?

The situation was a definite wake-up call. Clearly Reece was right. Maybe she had wallowed long enough in her 'unhappy misery', as he'd called it, and now she needed to bestir herself and fight for her marriage if that was what she really wanted. When she thought about being without Reece for the rest of her life, fear jackknifed through Sorrel's insides with such force that she felt quite ill. She had already lost her precious baby…to lose her husband—the love of her life as well—was simply too terrible an idea to be tolerated.

A star of Angelina's beauty and talent could probably get any man she wanted. *But Sorrel had only ever wanted Reece…despite what he might believe to the contrary.* So she would try her hardest to 'pull herself together'—the phrase made her heart bleed—and try to remind her disbelieving husband of the woman he had fallen in love with and married…*for better or for worse.*

The villa was quite compact and understated—beautifully decorated and appointed, but not the palatial residence that Sorrel had expected at all. It was more like a much loved home than a house that was only occupied by its internationally renowned owner very occasionally. And if the stunning Angelina welcomed Reece a little too warmly for his wife's liking, then she was surprised by the woman's equally enthusiastic welcome of Sorrel herself.

As they sat round in comfortable couches in the charming living room, every shelf and surface decorated with clearly personal photographs of family and friends, Sorrel stole a furtive glance at her husband. He was dressed in casual linen trousers and a plain white linen shirt that enhanced his tanned good looks with eye-catching compulsion. She longed for him to notice her as he seemed to be noticing Angelina. The Spanish star was dressed in dramatic red, her slinky low-cut dress clinging to every ripe curve, her dark hair swept up behind her head in an elegant and stunning chignon. When she moved, the slim gold bracelets on her wrist jangled and the air was permeated by her exotic perfume.

In her own little strapless blue sundress with the gauzy silver wrap shot with faint blue stars that Sorrel had added in deference to the invitation to dinner, she felt like a small grey mouse sitting next to a beautiful, sleek Siamese cat.

'Sorrel…I hope you did not mind me dragging you both away from your vacation to come and join me for dinner? When I found out that Reece was going to be here, I could not resist inviting you. As well as being the only promoter I would trust to oversee my concert tours, I much enjoy his company. He is always the perfect gentleman…always! Now, what can I get you to drink? A little wine, perhaps, before dinner? There will be just the three of us tonight, so you must both just sit back and relax. My housekeeper Pepe is preparing our meal, and he is the most divine cook!'

'Some wine would be lovely…thank you.'

'The same for me, thanks.'

As Reece added his own acceptance of some wine to

Sorrel's, Angelina excused herself and disappeared from the room to fetch it. The silence that fell in her absence was marked, and Sorrel all but squirmed with discomfort as she sat on the smart white leather couch and smoothed her palms awkwardly down the sides of her dress.

'If you'd rather I hadn't come with you tonight you should have said.'

At the hurt look in her eyes Reece bit back the cutting rejoinder that had immediately hovered on his tongue. If Sorrel had indicated even once that she would prefer him to refuse Angelina's invitation in deference to staying at home and trying to sort out their problems, he would most certainly have conceded to his wife's request. Even though at the time he'd told her they were going he had stated the fact in a tone that had brooked no argument. But she'd said nothing.

At the idea that she was likely building up more and more resentment towards him, and that the evening was bound to end up in another bitter argument, all Reece wanted to do right then was book the first available flight home. *But what would that solve?* Sooner or later they were going to have to come to some mutual agreement about their future. Reece wished his chest didn't feel as if it had been buried beneath the crushing rocks of a landslide at the thought, because it was becoming more and more clear that as far as he and Sorrel were concerned there might not *be* any shared future at all.

'I *wanted* you to come,' he said irritably, and felt mere inches away from snapping any second now if she so much as hinted at refuting that statement.

He despised himself for being so tetchy with her—

especially in light of all that she'd suffered—but he reminded himself that he had suffered, too, was suffering still. As his emerald gaze fell on her now, looking so pretty and enchanting in her simple blue sundress and sparkly stole, he longed to be able to take her somewhere private and kiss her—like he had kissed her the other morning, when he'd woken to find her sharing his bed at last. Of course since then she'd gone back to sleeping alone, and she would no doubt just push him away if he tried to make any kind of advance. *So much for making headway…*

'Reece…I really would like us to—'

Sorrel had to bite back her anxious attempt at conciliation when Angelina swept back through the door, carrying a bottle of wine and a tray of glasses. Once again the woman's sultry perfume and exotic presence impinged itself indelibly on the room like a colourful parakeet amid a flock of little brown sparrows. *Could Sorrel really blame Reece if his gaze turned to Angelina in admiration instead of to his wife?*

'By the way, I am sorry that my darling Emmanuel could not manage to stay awake to meet you, but he is only five years old and he gets so tired. You know how it is with little ones, yes?'

Turning her lovely dark eyes to Sorrel, Angelina couldn't know that that last sentence of hers had cut into her guest like a scythe cutting through corn. But as Sorrel lifted her wounded glance to Reece's she saw brief panic followed by regret mirrored in his own concerned gaze, and she let go of the breath she had inevitably sucked in hard and willed herself to release her pain…

'My sister has two small children, so, yes…I do know

how tired they can get.' Adding a smile to her words, Sorrel didn't see Reece relax his shoulders and some of the strain around his mouth gradually disappear.

Later on in the evening, after a superb dinner, Angelina declared that she wanted to show her guests around the charming well-kept grounds of her lovely villa. As they both stood up to join her, Sorrel asked to be shown where the bathroom was. Leaving Reece to accompany their hostess out into the balmy warm evening, she let herself into the immaculate bathroom with its shimmering sea-green tiles and marble basin, and thankfully shut the door behind her.

Dinner with Angelina as host had been surprisingly enjoyable and entertaining, and not nearly as great a strain as she'd anticipated it might be, but as the evening had worn on Sorrel had felt the inevitable tiredness creeping up on her. Glancing at her pale reflection in the mirror, she felt like a masked performer in a circus who, when the lights dimmed and the audience went home, was left with the less than sparkling face behind the mask.

With a little sigh she examined her watch and wondered how much longer they should stay before they could politely make their excuses and leave. Thinking about it now, she honestly would have liked to meet Angelina's little boy. Not because she wanted to wallow in the unhappy misery of not having a child herself—but because she was genuinely more comfortable in the company of children rather than adults.

Realising that she was missing the nephew and niece she had lived with for almost a month, Sorrel decided to ring Melody the next day and make arrangements to see them all as soon as she returned to the UK. And, after washing her hands in the bathroom basin, with some exquisitely scented soap that smelt like honeysuckle, Sorrel tidied her hair, reapplied some lipstick and went in search of her husband and hostess.

CHAPTER TEN

'SO YOU will think about what I said, *querido*? You know this means a lot to me.' Sorrel could hear Angelina petition Reece as they stood behind an intoxicating hedgerow of heavenly scented flowers. Her footsteps coming to a halt on the lamplit garden pathway, she flinched as though she'd been physically struck. *What was the other woman talking about so intimately with Reece?* Were her very worst suspicions coming true, and were they *really* having an affair? *Or were they simply on the brink of one?* Had things between her and Reece come to this sorry pass because she couldn't get over her grief about the loss of her baby and recognise that he had needs, too?

If Angelina *were* going to tour the States, and Reece agreed to promote that tour, then their paths would be thrown together almost daily. It would also mean that Reece would be away from home for months on end. *So much for a reconciliation and the possibility of renewing their marriage...*

'I promise to give it my serious consideration, Angelina,' Reece replied thoughtfully, and Sorrel heard a definite smile in his voice. 'That's all I can tell you right now, honey, but I'll definitely ring you in a few days.'

What was he going to give his proper consideration to? Sorrel fretted in panic. The possibility of having an affair with the beautiful opera star? Promoting her American tour? What?

Trying to hear herself think over the wild roaring in her ears, she took a deep shuddering breath, then walked forward to join her husband and hostess. The last thing she wanted Reece to accuse her of was lurking about in the shadows spying on him while he talked to Angelina. If she wanted to make matters ten times worse then that was definitely the way to go about it.

'Hi, there.' She smiled, deliberately keeping her voice light so as not to alert Reece to the fact that she'd inadvertently overheard some of their conversation.

Sorrel couldn't help noticing that the smile she'd heard in his voice when he'd spoken to Angelina was definitely *not* in evidence when he turned to regard her—his wife. Feeling ridiculously abandoned when he didn't reply to her greeting either, she shrugged her shoulders and turned to Angelina instead.

'Mind if I take a look around?' she asked, her feet already moving down the path away from her and Reece.

'Be my guest, my dear.'

Waving her away effusively, Angelina linked her arm through Reece's and, as easily as that, led him away in the opposite direction to his wife….

Sipping his Scotch, Reece walked out onto the terrace. The captivating scents of fragrant white lavender and red bougainvillea immediately entrapped his senses, so that he stopped for a moment simply to inhale the sensational heady fragrance more deeply into his lungs. Along with the luscious floral perfume that drifted up to him came the familiar sound of rasping insects mingling with the blessedly temperate night air.

Sorrel had long gone to bed, and out here on his own, thinking his thoughts and allowing relative silence to flow over him, Reece could finally exhale and give vent to his private frustration and pain over his marriage. *He would just have to give Sorrel her freedom.* What was the point in trying to hold onto a woman who clearly no longer cared for him? Somehow along the way they had lost touch with each other's needs and broken faith with the vows they had both voiced so passionately on the day they'd wed. Her eyes no longer lit up when Reece walked into the room, her mouth didn't immediately smile in welcome when he returned from his long trips away from home, and her manner and demeanour towards him—apart from the other morning, when she had briefly let him into her heart—were bordering on contemptuous…even more so since she had lost the baby.

Pressing the coolness of his glass against his heated forehead, Reece choked back a protesting groan and for a moment was completely gripped by the shudder of violent longing and regret that shivered through him when he thought about the baby they had lost.

Had it been a boy or a girl? *Don't go there,* his own silent voice warned him, briefly allowing the searing pain of the thought to grip him with a vengeance. Would the child have been as fair as Sorrel, maybe favouring the dark emerald of Reece's own eyes? Whatever their offspring had looked like, Reece would have loved him or her without reservation and with all his heart.

Would Sorrel consider trying for another baby with him? The wild clamour of his heartbeat almost deafened him. *Would she want to try again in spite of all that had happened between them?* Or was he destined to go through life without ever learning what it was like to be a father? Somehow he knew that would be a real tragedy. Of course he might eventually meet someone else, if he and Sorrel split up, have a child with them, but right now the idea was anathema to him.

He truly regretted that he'd never talked to his wife more about what she wanted from their union. If he was honest with himself he'd known all along she wasn't a typical career girl. Even the glamorous allure of the fashion business had not been able to captivate the interest of his lovely wife. She was her own woman, with her own ideas about how she wanted to live her life. And two things were now crystal-clear to Reece. One, she was clearly cut out to be a mother, and *not* a career girl or some pretty adjunct to her husband's career…. And two, *she clearly no longer wanted to be married to him.*

Tipping back his glass, Reece swallowed what was left of his whisky and welcomed the heated burn that slid so outrageously smoothly down into his stomach. He was not a man who gave up easily on anything he set his mind to, but it was a particular kind of torture to him to witness Sorrel walking around looking so unhappy. He couldn't do it to her. He couldn't make her stay with him when she was clearly wrestling with the idea that she might not want to.

So tomorrow they would talk about separating for good, and Reece would state his intention to gift her a generous provision of money and property to start her new future without him. When they returned to the UK they would revisit the offices of Edward Carmichael and Co., and Reece would instigate divorce proceedings as he'd originally been going to do. Then, when he'd told Sorrel his plans, he would telephone Angelina Cortez and accept her offer of promoting her new American tour. The tour would take him out of the UK for a year at least—by which time Sorrel would be much more settled in her new life and hopefully Reece would have gone some way to forgetting the beautiful blond angel he had married with such ludicrously high hopes…

'Reece?'

Her voice startled him so much that he almost dropped the glass he held in his hand. Turning slowly, he saw her standing between the opened patio doors, wearing a long ice-green silk nightdress and a matching robe. She'd left her hair loose and the ends lay in delightful rings of luxuriant curls about her slender shoulders, bright and glossy and infinitely touchable.

Frowning, Reece said nothing for almost a full minute. He was both perplexed and hypnotised by her sudden bewitching appearance when he'd been certain she'd been in bed asleep all this time.

'What is it?' he said finally, his voice sounding slightly rough. He knew it was the effects of both the whisky and his tiredness.

'Aren't you coming to bed?'

'Now, what *exactly* does that mean, Sorrel?'

Unable to keep the slight bite from his tone, Reece put his glass down on the concrete ledge behind his knees and dropped his hands to his straight, lean hips.

'It means are you coming to bed because I—?' She dipped her head, and if she hadn't been shadowed by the moonlight and the muted lighting round the terrace Reece would have sworn that she blushed as hard as any virgin. 'I'd like to come with you.'

Swallowing hard, Sorrel wished her heart wouldn't beat so fast, because it was causing a spinning sensation in her head that almost made thinking impossible. *Had she left it too late to try and make amends?* Reece's expression gave nothing away, his jaw implacable and the thoughts behind those arresting green eyes of his worryingly undetectable. *Was he thinking about the vivacious Angelina Cortez and wishing that it were her inviting him to bed instead of his wife?*

'And when did you decide that?'

He folded his arms across his chest in the white linen shirt that flattered his taut, lean musculature to perfection, and Sorrel caught the glint of the solid gold wristwatch that circled his tanned wrist. 'Please don't be so cynical,' she begged. 'This isn't easy for me, you know.'

Smoothing her hand down the sensuous silk of her robe, she couldn't help but shiver at the mockery that had been clearly evident in Reece's tone.

'What's the matter, Sorrel? Did you have another nightmare? That's all I'm good for, isn't it? Keeping nightmares away. Or are you of the opinion that it's *me* who causes them? Tell me—I'd really like to know.'

'Have you been drinking?'

Nervously her eyes darted to the empty glass Reece had left on the ledge. *It had been a totally stupid idea to come out here and expect him to jump for joy because she'd suggested she'd like to sleep with him tonight.* Now Sorrel could see that she had made a big mistake. She should have just left him to his whisky and his foul mood.

'What if I have? Go back to bed, Sorrel. Don't waste your time play-acting on my account. It's a little too late in the day to start trying to behave like a *real* wife, don't you think?'

The barbed insult—used once before to searing effect—hit Sorrel hard. She'd been genuinely intent on trying to meet her husband halfway. But, even though she was hurt, she stayed where she was, her jaw lifted and her blue eyes determined as she faced Reece out.

'I'm not "play-acting," Reece. I *want* to be a real wife to you. I know you have needs, too, and that—I—I haven't been considering them in the light of everything that's happened. I'm sorry that I've behaved that way, I honestly am.'

Swallowing down his initial resentment, Reece couldn't tamp down the flicker of hope that leapt into his heart at her surprising words. He'd fully expected her to engage him in another bitter, useless argument. But now, as he watched her standing there—looking so beautiful and with obvious hope in her eyes—he allowed his blood to heat without trying to immediately extinguish his desire because he assumed he hadn't a hope in hell of having it fulfilled.

'An apology? My, my…I didn't expect that.'

Although his words were faintly mocking, they weren't

cruel or dismissive, and a small sizzle of warmth settled inside Sorrel's stomach and wouldn't go away.

'Do you have any idea how much I ache for you? I swear to God you must have been put on this earth to drive me crazy.' He started to walk towards her. 'Do you know that?'

Shivering with the force of her own desire, Sorrel drew the sides of her robe together with trembling hands. Coming to a halt just in front of her, Reece was literally stopped in his tracks by the scent of a favourite perfume she wore, which he'd used to love. The warmth from her body seemed to reach out to him and make the ache that was already besieging him grip him so savagely that he almost swayed.

Unable to resist her charms any more than he could resist breathing, he considered her nervous blue gaze, and the peaches and cream complexion that was no less perfect from being scrubbed clean of make-up, and, using his thumb and forefinger to capture her jaw, impelled her startled face towards him. 'Do you really want to spend the night with me?' he asked, gravel-voiced.

'I…' Sorrel bit slowly down on her lip, hot colour pouring into her cheeks. 'Yes, I do.'

'Then let's go to bed, shall we?'

Surprising her, he lightly caught hold of her hand, then led her through the living room, out into the hallway and down the corridor to where the bedrooms were.

She took off her robe, laid it over a pink satin slipper chair in the corner of the room, and quickly climbed into bed. As she drew the covers up to her chest, Reece stood by the side of the bed and stripped off his shirt, quickly followed by his trousers. Already barefoot, he stood in front of Sorrel as God had made him—except for the white cotton boxers that sat low on his hips. *There wasn't a single inch of the man that wasn't totally pleasing to the eye.*

He'd always worked out a little, but basically Reece was one of those lucky individuals who had been born with more than his fair share of natural beauty. Whether he was sporting a tan or not, his sublime skin was smooth and supple and warm to the touch, with enough taut, sinewy muscle rippling underneath to make even the most inured female blush with pleasure.

Holding her breath, Sorrel cast her hungry gaze over his flat, perfectly proportioned stomach and—daring a little further south—caught a glimpse of the darker blond hairs that wove seductively down into his boxers.

Switching off the lamp by the bed, Reece finally divested himself of his underwear and climbed in beside Sorrel. The sheets were cool, but the temperature emanating from her husband's body definitely was not. Her skin began to tingle in anticipation. Even though she knew that she might have to live with her frustration at not being able to fully participate in their lovemaking, Sorrel was determined that she would show Reece that she was very much a 'real' wife when it came to the bedroom department. They might have sorted out zilch when it came to their relationship, but this was one area of their marriage that had always worked better than clockwork…the one area where communication had always been ten out of ten.

Lying back on the pillows, Reece drawled lazily, with a bad-boy smile, 'So now you've got me here…what do you intend to do with me?'

He was—did he but know it—setting the tone for what Sorrel had in mind.

Moving over to his side, she swept her hand deliberately sensuously down his chest to the flat of his stomach. Immediately she sensed his almost violent reaction. Then he went very still, and all Sorrel could hear was the sound of his slightly quickened breathing.

'Did you know…?' she said softly, letting the shoestring straps of her ice-green nightgown fall unchecked over her silky shoulders, exposing the darkened cleft between her breasts to his enraptured gaze. '…that there are more than seventy-two thousand nerve endings in your hands? Close your eyes…let me show you.'

Warming to her game, and to the unexpected sense of wicked anticipation that she was stirring inside him, Reece obediently shut his eyes. Lifting his hands, Sorrel placed his palms on her shoulders. She let them linger there for a moment, introducing them to the warmth and texture of her skin, then slowly, deliberately, guided them down to her breasts. She laid them on her tight aching nipples beneath the cool silk of her nightwear, biting her lip to control her own helpless desire to whimper and moan with pleasure at his touch. Then, when she sensed Reece's anticipation heighten, she pulled down the straps of her gown completely, exposing her bare breasts to the delighted and hungry exploration of his hands.

'See what I mean about nerve endings?' she whispered, leaning forward to lightly stroke down his face with her fingertips.

He opened his eyes and gazed fully on the sight of her flushed absorbed expression, and the beautiful pale breasts with their rosy tips that poured into his hands. *Her beauty almost undid him there and then.* The only destination of every red blood vessel in his body was *south*…right down to the tip of where Reece ached to feel Sorrel's touch the most.

'Let me kiss you,' he entreated, his voice no less than a grated hungry rasp.

Sorrel drew back with a teasing little smile around the edges of her lips. 'Not yet. *I'm* the one in charge…remember?'

Remembering with a groan, he momentarily protested as she moved his hands away from her breasts and slid them down past her waist to her hips. Then, when he'd anchored them fully either side of her, everything in him jumped to startled attention as Sorrel leant forward again and started to stroke her warm silky tongue over his nipples. Just when she'd captured his attention for life, she started to lightly lick down his chest to his stomach, and the lower her mouth travelled the more tense and hungry Reece grew.

Finally, when he didn't think he had it in him to hold out for even one more second without breaking out into a sweat, she took him into her mouth and Reece literally thought she was going to have to scrape him off the ceiling. Because of their sexual drought, Reece knew he couldn't hang on for long—but he also knew that he desperately wanted to pleasure Sorrel, too. So gently, carefully, he guided her back to him, whispering soft entreaties of need and want and finally capturing her lips with his and kissing her so hard that she whimpered between ragged breaths and fell onto his taut, flat stomach in helpless surrender.

'Now I want *you* on your back.'

Reece smiled, breaking contact momentarily, his lascivious green eyes making Sorrel feel as if she was going to melt into bliss right there. Then he manoeuvred her quite effortlessly into the position he wanted, his hands strong and determined.

It was *wonderful* to experience such intimacy again after so long, and Sorrel was only amazed that she had withstood the need for his touch for what now seemed like an eternity.

Stripping off her gown, he surveyed her semi-naked figure with a hot glance, a brief flare of regret and concern in his eyes as he regarded the black lace panties she was wearing.

'Are you OK?' he asked, his voice dropping to a near whisper.

As he asked the question, he stroked the flat of his hand across her smooth, ever so gently rounded stomach, and Sorrel thought she saw him wince. Knowing that he was thinking about the baby she'd lost, she swallowed down the intense pain inside her own throat and touched her fingers lightly to his sculpted, shadowed jaw.

'I'm fine,' she told him. 'I can't go all the way—but we can still give each other pleasure, can't we?'

'Sweetheart, your wish is my command. I'll pleasure you all night, if you want me to. And if that's not enough…then we've got all day tomorrow, too.'

But even as he joked with her, to take the sting out of the searing ache he felt inside, Reece knew that the innocence of their love had been nothing less than devastated by their shared experience of sorrow….

CHAPTER ELEVEN

LEAVING Reece to sleep in, the next morning Sorrel jumped in the car and drove to the little seaside market town on her own. It was the first morning she'd woken in a long time with something near to optimism in her heart.

Last night in bed Reece had been both loving and tender, and even though Sorrel had sensed a certain amount of reticence in him emotionally, she told herself that she'd been brave enough and determined enough to show him that she really *did* want to work at rebuilding their marriage. She hadn't let the sun go down on another row, or started another new day with more bad feeling and resentment.

Seeing Reece with a beautiful woman like Angelina had spurred Sorrel into the realisation that she still loved her husband deeply and didn't want their relationship to break up for good. She really couldn't tolerate even the thought of him being attracted to someone else, let alone marrying again if they divorced. Together, she told herself, they would find a way to make things work. They would explore solutions to meet their different wants and needs, and maybe attain a compromise that would satisfy them both. She could only hope and pray that it might be possible.

As she walked along the narrow uneven streets after purchasing some fruit and vegetables from the market stalls—taking her time to soak up the ambience and atmosphere—Sorrel lifted her face to the sun and felt her heart skip a beat at the idea of returning to the villa and seeing Reece again. She was planning on telling Ines that *she* would cook tonight, so their friendly housekeeper could have a night off. All she wanted to do right now was be alone with Reece and try and mend some bridges that had long been seared between them.

But when she got back to the villa and saw a gleaming Mercedes that she did not recognise parked in the front courtyard, Sorrel felt her heart skip a beat for a different reason. As she carried her straw bag of shopping towards the house, the happy sound of a child calling out fell on the air, quickly followed by the sound of delighted male laughter. *Reece.* Clearly they had visitors, but who?

Instead of going into the house, as she'd originally intended, Sorrel walked round to the back of the villa. And there on the beautifully kept sparkling green lawn she saw Reece throw a ball baseball-style to a small dark-haired boy in a checked shirt and red shorts. Sitting on a bench alongside, watching, was Angelina. Dressed from head to toe in white, with huge black sunglasses shielding her eyes, she looked just as if she'd stepped out of the pages of *Vogue* or *Marie Claire*.

Dry-mouthed, Sorrel caught Reece's eye and he waved—just as though everything was as it should be and absolutely nothing was amiss. But, apart from the blow she'd received at the sight of Angelina sitting there, Sorrel was also having trouble containing her emotion at seeing

Reece playing with the child...clearly Angelina's son Emmanuel. The thing that got to her was that he looked so heartbreakingly *natural* with the boy—as though it took no great effort on his part at all to be friendly or companionable with him. A shaft of pain moved through her at the idea that her own inability to carry a baby to term had deprived Reece of his own child...perhaps a *son*?

'Good trip?'

As Emmanuel chased after the ball, Reece's gaze moved possessively over his wife, and the smile he gave her showed he was genuinely pleased to see her.

'Fine.'

Unable to return his smile because of the torrent of jealousy that was flooding through her at the sight of Angelina, Sorrel deliberately glanced away. Her acknowledgement of the other woman was scant to say the least.

'Hello, there.'

'I hope you don't mind,' Angelina replied in her loud sing-song voice, 'but I had to come out this way today to visit a cousin of mine, so I rang Reece and asked him for your address. Emmanuel so loves to play ball, and your husband is so patient with him. He would make a wonderful father, no?'

'Excuse me.'

Clutching her bag of shopping tight to her chest, Sorrel started to move towards the house again. 'I've got to go and put some things away.'

In the bright kitchen she turned on the tap and filled a tall glass full of water. She drank it down, barely stopping to draw breath, perspiration sliding down her spine like honey down the side of a jar. *Had the Spanish star's com-*

ment about Reece making a 'wonderful father' been totally natural? A normal aside that anyone might make seeing the man and the small boy together? Or had it been a deliberate dig at Sorrel's inability to carry Reece's baby to term? Who knew what the two of them had discussed together…what secrets they had revealed? They seemed pretty close as far as Sorrel could tell.

Fear and jealousy swirled in her stomach, making her feel almost nauseous. Oh, why had the woman decided to visit her cousin nearby and invite herself over today of all days? Last night had been so good, and Sorrel had been hoping to spend the day alone with Reece, talking and making plans. Now everything was ruined.

'Sorrel… Oh, what a charming kitchen! Did you design it yourself?'

Suddenly Angelina was there at the door, appearing impossibly cool and elegant in her dazzling white, while in contrast Sorrel felt dowdy and hot and sticky in her blue shorts and lime-green sun-top—her hair making a determined bid for freedom from its mother-of-pearl clasp.

'I…er…no… That is…Reece and I discussed it with the Italian designers we hired.'

'Well, they did a fabulous job! You must let me have their number. Now, darling, I need to have a little chat with you.'

Laying her empty glass upside down on the drainer, Sorrel turned around reluctantly to give the other woman her attention. Her straw basket tipped over just then, and oranges and apples spilled out across the blond pine of the large kitchen table. Angelina captured an escaping orange and, laughing, put it in the carved wooden fruit bowl that stood nearly empty except for a very small bunch of grapes.

'I want to borrow your charming husband for the evening, if I may?'

Ignoring the disarrayed fruit, Sorrel tried to swallow over the suddenly harsh dryness in her throat. 'What do you mean?'

'I drove over to visit my cousin Alberto to ask him to be my escort tonight at a function I have been invited to. Unfortunately he has hurt his back and so cannot accompany me. This is not something I feel comfortable attending alone, so I was hoping that Reece could help me out. You do not mind if he comes with me, do you, *querido?*'

Feeling the immediate protest that surfaced from deep within lodge inside her throat, Sorrel shrugged. 'I am not his keeper, Angelina. If he would like to go, then he must go.'

'Si.' Angelina rose to her feet, her brief smile barely moving her lips. Clearly Sorrel's answer was not the happy response she'd expected. 'That is what I thought. Excuse me, but I must go and see what little Emmanuel is doing.'

Reece could understand Sorrel being upset with him about agreeing to accompany Angelina to the function she'd been invited to, but at the same time he would have thought that after last night she would know that there was no other woman he was remotely interested in sexually except her.

This was a one-off situation, and if Angelina's cousin hadn't hurt his back then it wouldn't have even arisen. He was going to be out for a few short hours and that was that.

But as he donned the tuxedo he'd brought with him in the hope that he and Sorrel might have something to celebrate before they returned home, he could feel no pleasure in the exquisite tailoring that he wore. If the truth was known, he was damned furious with Sorrel for making him feel guilty about something entirely innocent—something he was doing merely to help out a friend.

He walked into the living room to find her busy dusting a bookcase, with the books she'd removed from the shelves stacked up high on the coffee table beside her. There was a smudge of dust on her nose as she turned to regard him, and Reece couldn't deny the tug of need that arose inside him. It briefly doused his annoyance.

'What are you doing that for?'

Glancing up at the question, Sorrel felt her vision captivated entirely by the arresting sight of her handsome husband. She longed to tell him how good he looked—longed to plead with him not to go out tonight—but she was too afraid her plea might result in another soul-destroying argument. He clearly considered Angelina's needs to be more paramount than his wife's right now, and Sorrel would just have to bite her lip and accept it. *But the knowledge stung deeply.*

'I just thought I'd rearrange things a bit, that's all.'

'Ines would have done that for you if you'd asked her.'

'I wanted to do it myself. You know me...I *like* pottering around the house, smartening things up.'

'I know.'

Reece found himself smiling in spite of his admitted tension. Her assertion was another reminder that his wife was a natural-born home-maker. *Why hadn't he seen that so clearly before?* But right now he was remembering that her behaviour earlier, when their visitors were at the house, had conveyed to him her complete mistrust of the situation between himself and Angelina and he could hardly believe it. He'd been frankly furious that she'd been so deliberately unwelcoming to his friend and client. He didn't know if he could stand this blowing hot and cold behaviour of hers another second. His emotions were twisted inside out and that was a fact.

'I might be back late, so don't wait up for me.'

He glanced away, not wanting to kindle the fire of anger that he couldn't deny simmered inside him.

'OK.'

Hating her right then for what she was putting him through, Reece also knew a deep, underlying longing to regain the peace between them once more. *Last night had been so good.* He didn't want either of them to pour cold water on the warmth of their loving so soon. 'Look, I can change my mind. I can ring Angelina and tell her I'm not coming if you'd really prefer me to stay here?'

He saw the surprise in her eyes and breathed out when she briefly smiled. 'Don't be silly. I'm perfectly all right here until you get back. And I *do* trust you, Reece, so don't worry about that. I shouldn't have reacted the way I did earlier, and I'm sorry. I know that Angelina is only a client. Just go and have a good time, and in the morning you can tell me all about it.'

She picked up a book from the table and turned to place it on the cleaned shelf.

Staring at her exquisite profile as she positioned the book more carefully, Reece felt his stomach relax. He was relieved that she obviously regretted her earlier unsociable behaviour and was making an effort to be more reasonable—and if that was the case then maybe they *did* have a real chance to put things right?

'Well, don't stay up too late and tire yourself out. Get an early night. It would probably do you good.'

'I'm going to go to bed with a book and a nice cup of tea just as soon as I've finished this, I promise. Go on…you don't want to be late.'

Suddenly wanting to linger, Reece bent his head and briefly grazed her cheek with his lips. When he heard her soft, surprised gasp he had to muster all his will to force himself to go to the door and leave her there.

'Bye, then.'

As the door closed behind him Sorrel released a long, heartfelt sigh and dropped her head towards her chest. The sensation that remained from the touch of his lips against her cheek and the beguiling scent of his cologne that hovered in the air almost undid her right then—such was her almost uncontrollable longing for him. She really *did* want to trust him, but she was afraid she had just given him implicit permission either to continue or begin an affair with the beautiful Angelina…

Tossing and turning, Sorrel kicked off all the bedcovers and then, finally surfacing out of the fog of distress that had been enveloping her, sat up and examined the time on the bedside clock with her heart pounding. She'd had a dreadful dream about Reece and Angelina together—giving rise to her growing fear that they *must* be having an affair. Finding herself alone in their bed had her anxiety rapidly escalating, like wildfire ripping through a dense dry forest. Reece had told her he might be late, but three forty-five in the morning? Something *must* be going on!

Trying to calm herself, Sorrel glanced disconsolately towards the telephone. Had he tried to ring her and she'd slept through his call? Even now the dawn was starting to creep into the shadows, illuminating every corner of the bedroom from the uncovered window. Unable to contain her anxiety and impatience, she threw on her robe, then left the room to go down into the kitchen. On the way she took a quick peek into the bedroom further down the hall, just in case Reece had decided to sleep there so as not to disturb her. The room was worryingly empty.

As she made tea and brought her cup and saucer to the big pine table to sit down, she pushed her fingers agitatedly through her hair, wondering what on earth was keeping him so late. As her mind dived into the worst-case scenario—that he was spending a passionate night of torrid lovemaking with the sultry diva—it was all she could do to hold back her tears.

She shouldn't have waited so long to tell him that she loved him, she fretted, absent-mindedly stirring tea that she hadn't put any sugar in. If he *was* in bed with Angelina then Sorrel had *driven* him there. All right, the other night she had tried to show him how she felt—but what if he thought she'd made love with him out of guilt, because he'd accused her of being cold? Or, even worse, that she was intending to leave him again? Wasn't it only natural that he would seek solace in the arms of another warm and willing woman?

Finding it impossible to sit still even for a moment, Sorrel left her tea and went outside onto the terrace, to breathe in some early-morning air and watch the sun rise—her heart was almost bursting inside her chest at the thought that she might have left everything too late to make amends….

Everything had happened in a kind of surreal slow motion—like one of those dreams that seemed to last for ever but in reality only lasted for two or three seconds. Checking his mirror, Reece had been about to make a left turn when—seemingly out of nowhere, from the opposite direction—a black Porsche travelling at speed had crashed head-first into the right side of his car. *Angelina's side.* Fortunately for them both, the driver of the Porsche had hit the brakes as soon as he'd seen Reece's car, and the impact had not been as terrible as it might have been. But Angelina had still been badly hurt.

Right now the opera star was undergoing an operation to mend a broken leg and arm, and had several gashes to her beautiful face. She might easily have been killed. Not for the first time that shocking early-morning Reece sent up a prayer of thanks that he'd had the foresight to hire a car which had reinforced steel side impact beams in the doors. He was amazed and astonished that he didn't have a scratch on him himself. Of course he was grateful that he wasn't hurt—that he was still alive when the story might have been so different—but it didn't help him feel any less responsible for what had happened to Angelina…

A few hours later, having seen and talked to Angelina

in the recovery ward after a successful operation, and after assuring her that he would telephone the housekeeper who was taking care of Emmanuel, as well as her cousin Alberto to tell them the news, Reece procured himself a strong cup of black coffee and was shown into the doctor on duty's office to make his phone calls in private.

It was only as he finished making both calls that he finally allowed himself to think about Sorrel. About to pick up the receiver again and dial their number, he left it untouched in its cradle. She would be asleep in all likelihood, and she needed her rest. He didn't want to disturb her with news that might make her worry. It was probably wise to just let things be until he arrived home and could tell her to her face what had happened.

She came rushing out into the courtyard when she saw the unfamiliar red car pull into a space in front of the house. Realising straight away that it was a mini-cab, she stood dry-mouthed as she saw Reece disembark from the passenger seat and pay the driver. As the car pulled away, she stared at his unexpectedly dishevelled appearance. The dark shadow of stubble shading his jaw provoked all kinds of unpalatable suspicions, and she felt fear and nausea slam into her stomach all at once.

'What happened? I've been almost out of mind with worry!'

Wanting desperately to know the truth, Sorrel anxiously held back when he merely glanced at her with no emotion whatsoever, then proceeded to walk past her into the house. Her footsteps slowing, because her legs had suddenly turned as weak as water, Sorrel followed him inside.

In the kitchen he poured himself a glass of water and drank deeply. As she watched his throat convulse, Sorrel stared at him in near desperation.

'Reece? Tell me what happened? Why are you back so late? Were you with Angelina?'

'Of course I was with Angelina! Where the hell do you think I've been?'

So he admitted it? He'd been cheating on her, just as she'd suspected, and he wasn't even bothering to deny it!

'How could you? How could you do that to me?'

'What?' He stared at her as if she was someone he'd never seen before. 'What are you talking about?'

Sorrel could hardly breathe for the pain in her lungs. 'You spent the night with Angelina. I've been going crazy with worry, and all the time you've been in bed with that woman!'

'Where the hell did you get *that* idea?'

'What am I supposed to think when you didn't even ring me to let me know where you were or that you'd be so late? Instead you just walk in here in the early hours of the morning, looking like some lascivious, cheating—'

'Go on, Sorrel…why not go for the jugular? You were saying…?'

Something about the way his eyes were piercing her, and the edgy stance of his broad, hard-muscled shoulders beneath his tux, told Sorrel that something was very wrong here…and it wasn't what she thought.

'We were in an accident.' Reece's voice was low and harsh, his green eyes regarding her icily, frighteningly bitter. 'Another car hit us and Angelina was hurt. I've just come from the hospital…not her *bed*.'

Unable to stifle her gasp, and in spite of his austere expression, Sorrel automatically moved towards him. In response, Reece deliberately moved away from her. Trying to push aside her hurt and fear at his obvious rejection of the comfort she'd been going to extend—and at the colossal mistake she'd made as to the reason for his lateness—she nervously crossed her arms in front of her chest instead.

'Was she badly hurt?' she asked, small-voiced, wishing that she'd been far kinder to the other woman than she had been when she'd visited yesterday with her small son. Wishing too that she hadn't spoken in such appalling haste until she'd heard the facts.

Throwing her a look that said *What do you care?,* Reece replied, 'She has a broken leg and arm and some cuts to her face.' His face more grim than Sorrel had ever seen it before, he unknotted his tie and discarded it on the table. 'She certainly got more than she bargained for, going out with me last night.'

'Oh, God—I'm so sorry! And…and what about you? Are you hurt?'

'Not a scratch.' His mouth twisted in a black-humoured smile. 'Guess I must have a guardian angel.'

Clearly deriving no pleasure from the thought, he rubbed a weary hand round the back of his neck.

'I don't have time to stand here and row with you, Sorrel, so I'm warning you right now…don't even *think* about it. I don't think I can forgive you for such a *crass* insinuation, so I'm not even going to go there. I need a shower and a shave, and then I'm going to have to get to the police station to make a statement. Can you phone Ricardo and ask him if he'll come and pick me up?'

'Of course. But—'

He raised a dark blond eyebrow in warning. 'This conversation will have to be concluded some other time. And make no mistake…it *will* be concluded.'

Biting back her desperate need to apologise and beg his forgiveness for being so mistrustful, and her need to get him to talk about the accident—specifically about how he felt and what could she do to help—Sorrel nodded unhappily. He had to be feeling doubly bad because he had been driving Angelina, and she instinctively knew the burden of guilt would weigh heavily on him. She so wanted to alleviate that burden if she could. She loved him. He needed to know that.

But, because he looked so utterly bleak and so worryingly uninterested in anything she might have to say other than the bare minimum, Sorrel kept quiet yet again. 'I'll phone Ricardo right away. Why don't I make you some coffee before you go and shower? You look as though you need it.'

He stared at her as though her presence was too insignificant for him to acknowledge. 'I don't want any coffee. I don't want anything from you, as a matter of fact. All I want you to do is make that phone call and leave everything else to me.'

When he left the room it was as though an arctic chill had blown in that would never thaw in a million years….

Having visited Angelina for the second time that day, and witnessed the other woman's distress—first her shock and pain at the accident, and secondly her sadness at having to get her cousin and his wife to take care of Emmanuel, when she so desperately wanted to be with her child herself—Reece couldn't help but wish he'd said no to accompanying her to the dinner they'd gone to. *If he had, then this appalling nightmare would never have happened.* And Sorrel had had no right to accuse him of infidelity when he'd never even flirted with another woman—either in her presence or out of it—let alone slept with one!

He didn't think he could live with her suspicions or her anger towards him one more day. The car accident and the unpalatable accusations of this morning had left him feeling depleted and running on empty. *His life couldn't continue on such a soulless track.* He'd tried everything he could to get close to Sorrel, but she'd pushed him away almost at every turn.

On the drive home back to the villa, as he sat in the passenger seat beside his friend and gardener Ricardo, he already knew what he had to say to his wife. Maybe it was what she secretly wanted to hear and maybe it wasn't—either way, Reece convinced himself that ultimately it would be for her own good.

She wasn't inside the house, so Reece went in search of her out on the terrace. Lying in a sun-chair, wearing white linen shorts and an aquamarine sleeveless T-shirt, her feet bare, she looked lost in her thoughts as he arrived beside her. He was almost loath to disturb her. Telling himself that it was time he put them both out of this misery, he briefly touched her shoulder to get her attention.

When she removed her sunglasses and shielded her eyes with her hand to look up at him, the beauty of her dazzling blue gaze stirred such a torrent of longing inside Reece that he almost forgot what he'd been going to say to her.

'You OK?'

She'd been going to ask him the same question. 'I'm fine,' she replied warily, wondering whether the distant and frighteningly uncommunicative mood he'd been in when he'd left the house earlier had improved. She found herself clenching her stomach muscles hard as she waited to find out. 'Did everything go all right at the police station? How is Angelina doing?'

'I made a statement, and fortunately for me the guy driving the car that hit us accepted full liability. Told you I had a guardian angel.' An unusually self-deprecating smile touched his otherwise serious lips. 'As for Angelina…well, it's going to take some time for her to heal, but the doctors told me she's remarkably robust and her attitude is positive. All she can think of right now is getting back to little Emmanuel.'

A pang of kinship and compassion for the other woman vibrated through Sorrel. It was only natural that the singer's most urgent thoughts were for her child. It made her feel doubly bad that she'd been less than welcoming to her during her visit yesterday.

'Well, I hope she can be reunited with him soon. Who's looking after him? Her housekeeper?'

'No, her cousin and his wife. Thankfully Emmanuel knows them both quite well, so they're not exactly strangers.'

'But it's not like being with his mum.'

'Quite.'

Pacing a little, Reece dug his hands into his jeans pockets before turning slowly back to face Sorrel.

'I'll be visiting Angelina in the hospital over the next few days. Her manager is flying out this afternoon to see her, and no doubt the press will be hot on her heels if they're not already. I'll help out in any way I can.'

Feeling her chest inexplicably tighten, Sorrel waited for what was coming.

'I could come with you if you like?' she offered hopefully, wanting to distract him. 'Maybe I could even give Angelina's cousin a break and take care of Emmanuel for a little while?'

She would like that, she realised—the chance to get to know the little boy and maybe recompense his mother for her rudeness the other day…*not to mention her suspicions about her relationship with Reece.* But Reece was already shaking his head.

Taking his hand out of his pocket, he drove his fingers almost wearily through his dark blond hair. 'I want you to go back to the UK, Sorrel. Our vacation is over, I'm afraid. It's probably best if you go straight back to your sister's rather than home. I don't know how long I'll be here, and at least you'll have some company if you're with Melody. Besides that, I've got stuff backing up at work I need to take care of as well.'

'What if I don't want to go back to the UK? What if I want to stay here with you?' Knowing her voice sounded plaintive, Sorrel gripped the metal arms of the sun-chair a little too tightly. She saw him frown and take a deep breath, and her heartbeat almost came to a halt inside her chest.

'I don't want you to stay here with me, Sorrel. Remember what I said about concluding our earlier conversation? Well, I'm concluding it with my belief that as far as our marriage is concerned it's over. We gave it our best shot and it didn't work out…end of story.'

CHAPTER TWELVE

FEELING every bit of hope for their shared future turn to ashes, Sorrel stared at him in utter dismay. 'You don't mean that...you're upset over the accident, that's all. I don't want to go back home on my own, and I don't want to go to Melody's either. Now that this has happened, my place is with you.'

'If you truly believe your place is with me, why did you walk out on me three months ago?'

Alarmed that he had brought up something that she'd believed she had already adequately explained, and that he was still clearly bearing a grudge about it, Sorrel got up from the sun-chair to face her husband. 'I thought we'd been over all that? I told you. I left because you seemed far more interested in work than our relationship. OK, so I could have travelled with you indefinitely, but I wanted a home, Reece...a home and a family.'

There...she'd said it. Admitted that that was what she'd always hoped for with Reece. When the expression in his face didn't change or warm towards her in any way, an icy drip of fear seeped its coldness right into the very marrow of her spine.

'When a woman falls in love with a man it's only natural that she wants to have his child,' she pressed on. 'You were right…my heart wasn't in modelling—not one bit. It was an easy option for me, and I took it because it was there. I'm not ambitious like you are, Reece—but that doesn't make what I want wrong, does it?'

Had he ever made this woman really happy? Studying the sadness etched into her lovely face now, Reece knew a great desire for Sorrel to find joy again—and not just joy…peace, too. But he *too* needed to find peace. She had hurt him deeply with her accusations of his infidelity with Angelina and her evident lack of trust, as well as shutting him out of her life whenever it suited her. If fate dictated that she find that happiness with someone else then so be it—it was probably for the best. Even though everything inside him reacted vehemently with protest and hurt at the idea of her loving another man…bearing another man's children…Reece would let her go.

He sighed. 'I'm not suggesting that what you want is wrong, Sorrel. But I have to tell you that I can't deal with this ongoing misery between us any longer…*especially* since you've so clearly demonstrated that you have no trust in me whatsoever. It's better we go our separate ways and see if we can make a go of our lives either on our own or eventually perhaps with somebody else. I'd also urge you to get some help. I don't think things are going to get better for you until you do.'

'I don't want anybody else's help but *yours*.' Barely able to speak across the tension inside her throat, Sorrel glanced at him in despair. 'I'm truly sorry I acted so jealously, and didn't trust you with Angelina, but I acted out of insecurity about our relationship. I should have talked to you about it instead of just accusing you, but my confidence crashed after losing the baby and I couldn't think straight. Please forgive me! I went about things completely the wrong way and I regret it. You have no idea how much I regret it!'

'Maybe you do.' Reece's expression was strained, the pain of visiting even more distress on his wife as well as his own increasing agony cutting his heart in two. 'You won't want for anything, I promise you. I'll make you a good settlement that will give you choices, Sorrel. You won't ever have to worry about money. Go home and stay with Melody. I don't like to think of you being alone while I'm out here dealing with all this. When I get home I'll ring you and we can meet and talk properly. OK?'

'No, Reece. It's not OK.' Her mouth wobbled treacherously. 'How *could* it be OK when you're planning on walking away from something that started out with so much hope?'

A flash of deep regret blazed momentarily in Reece's dark emerald gaze at her impassioned words. 'That was *then,* Sorrel. You know as well as I do that things have changed too much for us ever to reclaim what we had when we were first together. I'm sorry, but I can't talk about it any more now. I've got Angelina to think of in hospital. Please, honey. Go home and stay with Melody. Promise me?'

Perhaps it was unreasonable of her to feel aggrieved and torn up with jealousy because he was putting a client's welfare before his wife's needs yet again—especially when Angelina had suffered an accident and was lying injured in a hospital bed—but Sorrel told herself she was only human. If Reece had accepted her offer to stay and help him deal with this thing then there would have been no need for her to feel so rejected or despairing. *But he'd told her that in his opinion they'd given their marriage their best shot and it hadn't worked. And now he wanted to call it a day. Just where was she supposed to go from such a heartbreaking premise?*

Unable to speak because of the upsurge of pain inside her chest, Sorrel warred desperately with herself to not break down in front of him. When she knew that she was very definitely losing the battle, she turned and ran back inside the house….

'So, we'll get some samples made up and take it from there. Well done, Sorrel…these are really terrific. I'm so glad you've kept working on them.'

Nina slid the drawings back into the leather-bound art portfolio and laid it on top of her desk in the back room of her exclusive boutique. For once not denying herself a deep satisfaction and sense of accomplishment at what she'd been trying so hard to achieve, Sorrel smoothed her hand down the tailored jacket of her black trouser suit and took a small sip of the tea she had almost allowed to get cold in her nervousness at Nina's expert opinion of her latest fashion drawings.

If the samples she was going to get made up caught the eye of an experienced designer, it was highly possible that—coupled with her own inside knowledge of the fashion industry from her years as a model—Sorrel was going to find herself with a brand new career. Since returning from Portugal she had worked late into the night almost every night for the past two weeks, fine-tuning and improving her designs, so the news that her diligence had been successful was nothing less than wonderful. The best news she'd heard in ages.

If only she had been able to share it with Reece it would have been all the sweeter....

'Come on, guys, give Auntie Sorrel a break. You've been monopolising her all day and now it's *my* turn! Besides…it's time for bed. Pop upstairs and get ready, and I'll come and kiss you goodnight in a few minutes.'

'Goodnight, Auntie Sorrel,' Will and Daisy intoned one after the other, and—for once not protesting—they started to gravitate towards the door.

As five-year-old Daisy yawned and rubbed her eyes, Sorrel experienced a wave of love so powerful that she had to practically sit on her hands to stop them from reaching out and pulling the child to her for another cuddle. Both children resembled a couple of golden-haired angels, and as far as Sorrel was concerned it was almost impossible to deny them anything. Consequently she had been playing games and drawing pictures with them for most of the day—and she hadn't minded a bit.

The rain had started first thing, and hadn't let up, but with Sorrel keeping the children occupied at least Melody had been able to get on and shop and cook and do all the things she needed to do on a Saturday. Now, as she called out, 'Goodnight, darlings…I love you!' as the children left the room and trooped upstairs, Sorrel immediately felt the old emptiness inside her spread out inside her chest with a force that took her breath away. *Because she wasn't with Reece. He could have died in that car accident, and he would never have even known the depth of her love for him.* And instead of telling him how she'd felt, she'd wrongly accused him of spending the night in another woman's bed.

The thought startled her, like an old adversary she thought she'd vanquished sneaking up on her and knifing her cruelly in the ribs. He'd rung her only once in the whole fortnight she'd been with Melody, and that had been to tell her that Angelina was now out of hospital and recuperating at her villa. Her cousin Alberto and his wife were helping to take care of her and her small son. As for himself, Reece was staying on indefinitely to do some business in Lisbon and didn't know when he would be back in the UK. His voice had sounded distant in every way, and not just because he was in a different country from Sorrel.

Did he think it would make things easier for her if he maintained the aloof formality of a practical stranger when he spoke to her? Did he have no clue that he'd broken her heart into a thousand little pieces? Pushing away the wave of despair that threatened, Sorrel reminded herself of her newfound determination to win him back. Since getting back to the UK she had paid two visits to a bereavement counsellor, enrolled in some exercise classes at Melody's local gym, and started to eat properly again. And each day she saw a distinct improvement in the gaunt face that stared back at her in the bathroom mirror. She actually had some colour in her cheeks again, and the waistbands on the skirts and trousers which had started to swim on her were once more starting to fit her properly. Coupled with her industry in working on her designs, and the success she had won because of it, her confidence and esteem were slowly but surely returning.

Any day now she was going to ring Reece and ask if they could meet. She'd already rehearsed a thousand times what she was going to say to him when she saw him. She would leave him in no doubt that she loved him with all her heart—had never *stopped* loving him even when things were at their worst—and wanted the chance to try again. She would apologise profusely again for not trusting him, for being so stupidly jealous and insecure, when in reality he had never given her a moment's cause to act in such a manner, and she would show him that she had the strength and determination to rise above all her heartache and embrace life with both hands again. And if she *failed* to win him back, even though she told him that she loved him, then at least she wouldn't have walked away from her marriage without a fight for its survival.

Wrapped up in her thoughts, Sorrel barely noticed Melody walk in behind her until she stooped and affectionately ruffled her hair. 'How about a gin and tonic? I'm sure you could do with one after all your hard work. I know *I* could—and I've been child-free all day, thanks to you!'

'I'll keep you company, then…thanks.'

Sorrel's smile was genuinely warm. Her sister had been so good to her, letting her stay in her house and giving her space when she needed it, as well as encouraging her in her efforts to come to terms with her tragedy and improve her life. Not for the first time she felt immensely grateful that she had such a supportive and loving family.

'You know…if you hadn't decided to give Britain's top designers a run for their money with those fabulous designs of yours then I'd definitely be suggesting you move in permanently as my nanny! All my children talk about is "Auntie Sorrel this…Auntie Sorrel that…" You can't put a foot wrong as far as they're concerned.'

'What can I say except that I love kids? It's easy to make them happy. All you have to do is love them with all your heart.'

Melody went very quiet at her younger sister's words, and Sorrel was taken aback to see moisture glistening in her eyes. Ever practical, Melody was not one for frequent displays of emotion, so the sight was all the more startling.

'You know what? One day you're going to have a houseful of wonderful children—and Will and Daisy's noses are going to be put thoroughly out of joint when you do!' she said, wiping her eyes with the back of her hand.

'No, they won't. I'll always have a special place in my heart for those two. Now, how about that gin and tonic you promised me? A girl could get very thirsty waiting for service in this house!'

As Melody laughed and went to fix their drinks, for a moment or two Sorrel allowed herself to lapse into her favourite daydream of becoming a mother. And when she thought about who she wanted to be the father of that 'houseful of wonderful children' Melody had mentioned she was in no doubt as to *exactly* who would fit the role.

Sitting outside in the car, Reece studied the picturesque country house, with its model sailboats in the windows and its blue and white frontage, and had to take a deep breath to bolster his courage before he got out and knocked on the door.

He should have rung first to make sure she was there. But he hadn't been able to face returning straight away to the house in Pimlico, to feel the emptiness of the rooms press in on him like the moving dungeon walls in those old black and white movies that threatened to crush the unfortunate victim who was trapped within them. *Which was what it would have been like without Sorrel.* He'd decided to chance his luck instead, and had driven straight to Melody's from the airport.

Now, as he flexed his fingers around the leather-covered steering wheel of his Jaguar, he told himself not to expect too much. There was no guarantee that she'd even want to speak to him. He'd been so wrapped up in his own pain that day he'd told her to go that he'd probably demonstrated about as much sensitivity towards her needs as an impervious elephant standing on a butterfly. That as soon as she'd left Portugal to fly home the truth had dawned on him with all the brutal finesse of a giant brick falling down on his head. *He was making a terrible mistake in letting her go. She meant everything to him...always had, always would.*

So much had happened to prevent him from thinking clearly. First the problems within their marriage that he hadn't known how to fix, then Sorrel losing the baby, and Reece being involved in the car accident and seeing Angelina get hurt, then Sorrel's hurtful accusations about his fidelity. For a while he'd done nothing but wallow in his own misery and pain. But now his thoughts were razor-sharp. He wanted his wife back in his life for *good.*

Not wanting to delay seeing her for one second more, he climbed out of the driver's seat, slammed the door behind him and walked up to the front door of the house. There were a couple of small bicycles with stabilisers standing to the side on the gravel, along with a striped toy buggy and a bright orange football. Something about the very ordinary sight that denoted a family lived there struck Reece with forceful realisation. He was in no doubt that that was what he wanted, too…a family.

Melody answered the door dressed in jeans and a white shirt, with a single string of white pearls round her neck. She was a pretty woman, with a fresh-faced 'outdoorsy' look about her, but next to Sorrel her undoubted attractiveness paled to the merely ordinary.

'Hi.'

He unleashed one of his most destroying jaw-dropping smiles, did he but know it, and for a full second Melody opened her mouth to speak and nothing came out. Then, quickly gathering herself, she frowned a little and stepped back inside the hall to let him in.

'She's in the living room. Do me a big favour, Reece? She's worked hard to start rebuilding her life…don't go and ruin things for her, will you?'

Flushing a little beneath his tan, Reece nodded briefly before brushing past her and heading towards the living room.

Still sitting amongst the children's toys on the carpet where she'd been playing with her nephew and niece earlier, Sorrel was flicking through a pad of Daisy's drawings when she happened to glance up and to her utter amazement and shock saw her husband standing in the doorway. Golden-tanned and golden-haired, his long legs encased in dark blue denim and wearing a fitted black sweater that could not hide the impressive musculature underneath, the sight of him stirred a heat inside Sorrel that touched to tinder would blaze into an inferno. She could hardly catch her breath for the need and longing that engulfed her.

'What are you doing here? Why didn't you phone to say you were coming?'

'I wanted to see you…I can't do that on the phone.'

That slow melting drawl of his, along with the hotly examining glance that he swept over her face and body, made the blood in her veins all but bubble. Unsure of how to respond, Sorrel rose slowly to her feet, dusting the seat of her jeans as she straightened, then absently fingering a button on her cream blouse as she regarded Reece more closely.

'I—I was going to ring you myself. We need to talk and I—' She broke off from what she'd been going to say because her husband was studying her intently…almost as though he'd never seen her before.

She looked like a million dollars…what had she done to herself? No other woman could make a pair of jeans look classier or more sexy than Sorrel, Reece was thinking, as every muscle he owned tightened and throbbed and his blood could think of only one direction in which to travel. But today she took both those descriptions to new heights. Not only that…but when she'd been sitting there, amongst the detritus of Will and Daisy's toys, she'd looked like *home* to him—more than any *place* or any *house* or any country in the world he might visit. *She* was where he wanted to be…not just now, but for every single remaining day of his life.

He shrugged and smiled. 'I agree we need to talk, but I haven't come to discuss divorce, if that's what you're thinking.'

'Then what *have* you come for, Reece?'

He shifted from one booted foot to the other, looking as if the words he wanted to say were frustratingly eluding him. 'I've come to apologise to you for the way I've behaved and to ask your forgiveness.'

'You have?' Her blue eyes considered him with definite surprise.

'Do I have it?' he pressed, more quietly.

'Oh, Reece, I—'

'Wait…let me finish.' He held up his hand. He had to reach deep inside himself to try and articulate what was in his heart, but articulate it he would. 'I want you back, Sorrel. I should never have pushed you away like I did after the accident, but I was mad as hell that you'd accuse me of sleeping with Angelina when just the night before we'd spent the most amazing time together.'

He saw her colour profusely at the recollection and her reaction gave him hope. 'I need you. I can hardly contemplate going through another day without you. I can't get you out of my thoughts for even a second. Don't you know that?'

'Well, I—'

'I'm truly sorry, baby. I didn't mean to be so cold when you told me you were pregnant. I didn't really know what having a baby meant to you then, and even if you'd told me I don't think I'd have listened. It was only after you had the miscarriage that I realised the importance of the life we had lost…the precious chance to be a family.'

She looked stunned, her blue eyes focusing intently on him as though she couldn't quite believe what he was saying.

'And I don't blame you for how you acted towards me after losing the baby either. I should have been more understanding, but I was impatient for your love. I was afraid you were withdrawing so much inside yourself that I'd never find you again…that soon you wouldn't need me at all. That scared me to death, Sorrel. And now all I want you to do is to come home with me.'

'Back to London, you mean?'

'We have a house there, don't we? But if you don't like it where we are…if you want us to buy another place somewhere else…all you have to do is tell me.'

'You'd be willing to do that?'

He'd be willing to live any damn place in the world so long as she was beside him. Why wasn't he getting through to her?

'Whatever makes you happy, sweetheart. That's all I want from now on.'

His words brought a joyous, uninhibited smile to her beautiful lips. Light and hope went rushing through Sorrel's bloodstream as if she'd been injected with pure golden sunshine. *The sensation was making her almost delirious with happiness.*

'I want to make you happy, too, Reece! That's what I wanted to talk to you about! All those things you said…I feel exactly the same way. And home isn't an address, as far as I'm concerned…my home is wherever *you* are.'

'You mean it? I couldn't stand it if you were just saying that to placate me. If we're going to make our marriage work, there has to be absolute honesty, absolute trust. Do you agree?'

Seeing the ghost of pain still lingering there at the edges of his mouth made Sorrel yearn to go to him, to hold on tight and never let go.

'I agree…with all my heart.'

'Can you forgive me for being such an all-time jerk? I love you, Sorrel. You're my life… No success I can achieve means anything to me without you to share it. The only achievement I really want is a happy, successful marriage with you. Is there any chance you might want to meet me halfway?'

'No.'

'What?'

The hope that had appeared as he was speaking faded from his eyes in an instant. But Sorrel couldn't stop herself smiling as she went towards him, her heart imbued with so much love that she was practically floating. *He loved her! He really loved her!*

'I *don't* want to meet you halfway, Reece. If we get back together I'm afraid you've got my one hundred per cent commitment to making this relationship work—and I want the same from you. It's got to be all or nothing, because I just won't settle for anything less.'

'That sounds like a pretty good deal to me. I'd be a fool not to take it, don't you think?'

'You're anything but that, Reece…and I can't live without you either. I was so afraid when you said we'd given it our best shot and it hadn't worked.'

'I must have been crazy. I was mixed up and frustrated. I've made some wrong choices in my life, God knows, but that had to be the worst. However, now that I've got you back, I'm never going to let you go again.'

Making no ceremony about pulling her hard against him, Reece tantalised her with his mouth almost unbearably, by pausing bare inches from her startled lips. Sensing his heat and desire, Sorrel was almost faint with longing, waiting for his kiss.

'Is that a promise?' she asked weakly.

'On my life,' he replied, just before his mouth touched hers….

The stunning blonde—her silk chiffon dress clinging lovingly to her amazing body, her long slender legs tanned with the kiss of golden sun and her feet displayed in gold diamanté sandals with a killer heel—drew his attention as devastatingly as she drew the attention of every other male in the vicinity. He could sense them all practically swallow their breath as she turned from contemplating the picture above the fireplace to make an interested inventory of the rest of the stunning lobby, with its vast crystal chandeliers and exquisite furnishings.

As her unbelievably crystal blue eyes moved casually round the room, they alighted all of a sudden on his own magnetised gaze. As his mouth turned dry as sand and his heart began to thud heavily inside his chest, she slowly and deliberately moved towards him—almost gliding, with a provocative little sway of her perfectly slender hips—and never had a woman epitomised the phrase 'poetry in motion' more.

'I saw you looking at me.'

Stopping in front of him, she let her eyes dip purposely, flirtatiously, then lifted them in slow, bold contemplation of what he knew must be his frankly dazzled expression.

'And I liked what I saw.'

His confession was equally bold, and, allowing his hungry gaze to linger on the sexy décolletage of her dress, he lifted the curling blond tendril that glanced against the side of her jaw and examined it, thinking that the touch of the most exquisitely perfect silk in the world could not possibly match it for sensation. *He wanted her so badly that his whole body was swept up into one aching, throbbing vortex of desire and need.* So transfixed was he by her beauty and the spell it cast around him that truly all his life seemed to spin right down to this one incredible moment, when the only two people who existed in the world were him and her.

'I'm waiting for someone.' Dropping her voice to an almost-whisper, she lightly brushed her hand against his hip.

Sweet Lord, have mercy…

'So am I,' he came back, bolder now, letting his fingers wrap possessively around her small-boned wrist. 'And I think I've just found her. Do you want to go somewhere?'

'You're staying at the hotel?' He heard the slight catch in her voice—the delicious nuance of forbidden thrill and anticipation—and a cascade of hot little shivers imploded all the way down his spine.

'I am. Will you come up to my room?'

'What could possibly be so interesting up in your room?' she teased, blue eyes like melting crystals as they danced coyly back at him.

'Are you the kind of woman who likes to play with fire? Who doesn't mind getting…*hot*?'

Her quick blush told him all he needed to know. Needing no more confirmation than that, he took hold of her hand and led her to the other side of the spacious lobby, where the elevators were.

All the air was punched from her lungs when he kissed her. Hot, sweet, dazzling sensation flowed over her and left her feeling as though her feet no longer touched the floor. She hardly knew where they were going as his strong arms propelled her with him across the darkened room.

The long, diaphanous white curtains at the two large windows were being teased by a gentle breeze from outside, and the only illumination of any kind came from the moonlight. She was so turned on by this game they were playing that she felt as if she was melting. It had been Reece's idea to drive straight to one of London's most ravishing hotels and stay the night instead of going straight home. It had been his idea for them both to dress up, and for him to 'pick her up' in the lobby—as though they were passionate strangers who'd glimpsed each other across the lobby and couldn't contain their wild unfettered attraction.

Now, with each passing tension-filled moment, Sorrel could hardly wait for him to possess her again—hungrily and without restraint, like he'd done in the early days of their passionate courtship.

'Take off your dress,' he ordered, his glittering green eyes devouring her as he released her and pushed her towards the bed.

His commanding tone of no compromise secretly thrilled her.

'I thought you liked me wearing this dress?' she teased, suddenly more shy than she would have believed possible. But right now Reece was like a sexy stranger she was discovering all over again.

'I like it just fine,' he drawled, hands on his hips. 'But I like what's underneath it much better.'

Obliging him, Sorrel swept her dress up over her head, then carelessly discarded it on the brass rail of the big double bed behind her. Standing there in her lacy white underwear, with Reece's gaze touching her everywhere, she felt sexy and feminine and *loved* for the first time in what seemed like years.

'Now take off the rest,' he told her, a predatory smile settling unashamedly on his fascinating lips.

Feeling all the blood rush to her head, Sorrel silently stripped for him, then stood there looking at him for long seconds, begging him with her eyes to make love to her.

'I'm cold.' She shivered, crossing her arms in front of her chest, and silently, without preamble, Reece all but tore off his own clothes and came to her, tipping her headlong onto the bed behind them.

When his hard strong body settled over hers, they were both too needy and excited to delay gratification a moment longer. Wrapping her long legs around his taut, hard middle, Sorrel tipped back her head and let out a long low moan as he filled her with his erection—sliding into her with one lingering, scalding stroke that sent her blood racing round her body like a blaze that burned totally out of control.

'I love you,' she whispered into his ear as he started to move rhythmically inside her. His silky hair brushed against her cheek, and the shadow that had started to form around his chiselled jaw was scratchy and slightly rough against her softer more feminine skin, but Sorrel loved every touch as though experiencing it for the very first time, and didn't want it to stop.

'I love you, too, my angel,' Reece grated back to her, his voice warm and husky with passion and need.

He drove into her like a man held deep in the power of some irresistible mystical enchantment, and Sorrel shuddered as her tight, hot muscles possessively claimed him, her eyes filling with helpless scalding tears that streamed down her face as she climaxed—the unbelievable intensity of forceful sensation taking her to a heavenly stratosphere never visited before and bringing her back down to earth again with dizzying slowness.

Kissing her tears away with great tenderness, Reece moved his mouth down to her breasts, teasing and licking and suckling, until finally lifting his head as his body shuddered violently and he spilled the climax of his loving deep inside her.

'We didn't use anything.' Her blue eyes wide and her lovely face even paler in the soft trail of moonlight that illuminated the bed from the window, Sorrel felt her breath momentarily suspended as she glanced up at Reece.

'It's no good using protection if we want to make babies, honey.' His tone was gently mocking, but his emerald eyes couldn't have been more serious.

Her heart almost burst from her chest. 'I'm not trying to make you be something that you don't want to be,

Reece,' Sorrel assured him softly. 'It was wrong of me to try and push you into being a father when I knew you didn't want to be. It doesn't matter if we don't have babies. Children are important to me, but I wouldn't want to lose you. I'll go with you anywhere you want me to go, as long as we can just be together.'

Knowing that she meant it, Reece felt his love for this woman deepen even more than he'd thought possible. *But he didn't want Sorrel to make any more sacrifices for him.* Especially not now, when he knew for certain that he wanted a family, too. He might have been injured or even killed in that car accident, and when he'd survived both catastrophes he'd figured that he must really have a guardian angel.

Remembering back to that day in the beautiful Portuguese church, when he'd thought he'd smelled roses—his mother's favourite perfume—Reece wondered if his mother might be that guardian angel. Considered too that she had been silently giving him her blessing and trying to give him the message that children were the most precious of gifts. *He'd been spared from that accident for a reason.* And Reece was now convinced that that reason was Sorrel and their future family…

'Wherever you are is home to me, Sorrel…I mean it. I didn't think about you having to spend so much time alone when I was working. And it was wrong of me to expect you to follow me around like some rootless gypsy…especially when I wasn't prepared to listen to what you really wanted. I'm sorry, sweetheart. And you're *not* making me be anything I don't want to be. I *want* us to have a family together. I was honestly devastated when you lost the baby.'

'Reece…' Pulling his head down to hers, Sorrel tenderly touched her mouth to his, her heart so full she could barely find words for what she wanted to say. 'You're going to make the best father *and* husband…I just know it.'

'Then let's not waste any more time making that a reality, huh?'

His wicked smile a mixture of angel and devil, Reece silenced anything else she might be going to say with a kiss that melted her right down to the very marrow in her bones….

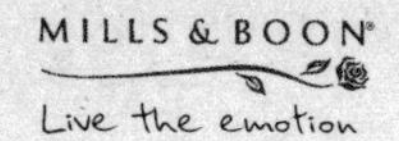

0406/01b

Modern romance™

BOUGHT FOR THE MARRIAGE BED
by Melanie Milburne

Nina will do anything to keep her twin's baby from harm. So when Marc Marcello wants to take his brother's child, Nina lets herself be bought as Marc's bride instead. But what price can be placed on her…in his bed?

THE ITALIAN'S WEDDING ULTIMATUM
by Kim Lawrence

Alessandro Di Livio always protects his family, even seducing gold digging Sam Maguire to keep her away from his brother-in-law! But when passion leads to pregnancy, Alessandro wants to keep Sam as his wife – and their baby as his heir!

THE INNOCENT VIRGIN *by Carole Mortimer*

Abby Freeman is thrilled when she gets a job as a TV chat show host, and who better to grill than famous journalist Max Harding? Max is happy to let Abby get close – but only in private. How can Abby get the story…without losing her innocence?

RUTHLESS REUNION *by Elizabeth Power*

Sanchia has amnesia but when Alex Sabre recognises her, she realises they once knew each other intimately. To unlock her past Sanchia must spend time with Alex. What happens when she learns the truth about the man she's falling in love with…again?

On sale 5th May 2006

Available at WHSmith, Tesco, ASDA, Borders, Eason, Sainsbury's and most bookshops

www.millsandboon.co.uk